### PATIENT REVENGE.

"I'm going to take him, Lisette. Not now, not yet, because here, on this ship, I'm as helpless as you are. So I'll smile with him and eat with him and drink with him and let him dream of all the things he's going to do to me after I've served my uses. Then, one day, I'll take him. I'll strip him down, stitch by stitch, till there's nothing left but his yellow soul and his white slug's body. Then I'll kill him for you."

**THE CONCUBINE**

# THE CONCUBINE

## Morris West

BANTAM BOOKS
TORONTO · NEW YORK · LONDON · SYDNEY

*This low-priced Bantam Book
has been completely reset in a type face
designed for easy reading, and was printed
from new plates. It contains the complete
text of the original hard-cover edition.*
NOT ONE WORD HAS BEEN OMITTED.

THE CONCUBINE

*A Bantam Book / published by arrangement with
William Morrow & Co., Inc.*

PRINTING HISTORY

*This title was previously published as a part of A WEST QUARTET by
William Morrow, September 1981*

*Bantam edition / June 1983*

ISBN 0-553-23305-X

*Published simultaneously in the United States and Canada*

Bantam Books are published by Bantam Books, Inc. Its trademark,
consisting of the words "Bantam Books" and the portrayal of a rooster,
is Registered in U.S. Patent and Trademark Office and in other
countries. Marca Registrada. Bantam Books, Inc., 666 Fifth Avenue,
New York, New York 10103.

PRINTED IN THE UNITED STATES OF AMERICA

O      0 9 8 7 6 5 4 3 2 1

# THE CONCUBINE

# Chapter One

When he woke, it was midafternoon.

The first thing he saw was the old-fashioned fan turning slowly and uselessly in the heavy air. It made no draft, only a sleepy drone as if the spindle were worn and needed oiling. Then he saw the sunlight seeping through the slats of the rattan blinds.

It was enough for a beginning.

He was in bed, in a room with a fan. It was daytime. The rest could wait until he was strong enough to cope with it. He closed his eyes again. His mouth was dry and there was a bitter, metallic taste on his tongue. His skin was clammy and strong-smelling. When he tried to move, his muscles were slack and reluctant.

He remembered that he had had the fever.

He wondered, idly, how long the attack had lasted and whether anybody had come to look after him. There must have been someone. His clothes had been stripped off and he was naked under the cotton sheets. There had been vague voices and hands mopping his forehead, holding him up while other hands held a glass to his chattering lips. Hands and voices, but never a name or a face.

Carefully, he opened his eyes and turned his head. He

saw a bedside table of red carved wood, a glass jug, half full of water, and a tumbler. He eased himself into a sitting position and poured himself a drink. His hand trembled and the jug rattled against the tumbler and some of the water splashed onto the tabletop.

The drink disappointed him. It was warm and flat and the bitter taste was still in his mouth when he had finished. He put down the glass and began to take stock of the room: a long casement window shaded with bamboo blinds; white walls; a hanging cupboard, a dressing table, a writing desk, all of the same red wood; a sea-grass chair, with a cushion covered in batik; two doors, one of them carrying a framed notice.

Now he remembered the rest of it.

He was in a hotel—the Tanjil Hotel in Djakarta. He had flown in from Pakanbaru in Sumatra. The fever had hit him an hour after his arrival—a wrenching, shivering agony ending in darkness. His name was Mike McCreary. He was an oil man out of a job.

He drank another glass of water, then threw back the sheets and slid off the bed, steadying himself against the table until the first giddiness had passed. Then he walked slowly across the polished floor to the bathroom. From the shaving mirror a gaunt yellow face stared back at him: an Irish face, with bright, shrewd eyes sunk deep in their dark sockets, an inquisitive nose and a wide, thin mouth that grinned engagingly when he was happy and closed like a trap when the black mood was on him, as it was now.

For McCreary was on the beach, flat broke and busted, a long, long way from Kerry of the Kings.

He shaved unsteadily but carefully and rubbed his face with astringent. Then he turned on the shower and stood a long time under the jets, lathering and sluicing, until the fever reek was gone from his skin and he felt fresh again. Then he walked back into the bedroom and stood towelling himself, naked under the reluctant, droning fan. No sooner was he dry than the dank heat made him sweat again, and after a while he gave it up and began to dress, whistling an off-key version of "The Raftery Little Red Fox," which is a song made in Kerry by the great Raftery, himself a footloose, wandering man.

There was a knock at the door. McCreary stopped whistling and called, "Come in." The door opened and Captain Nasa stepped into the room.

He was a small, compact Javanese with an oblique smile and a soft voice. He was dressed in a grey tropical suit of military cut and he wore a black fez cocked at a slight angle. He closed the door behind him and bowed stiffly.

"Good afternoon, Mr. McCreary."

McCreary said, "Good afternoon," and went on knotting his tie. Captain Nasa took out a cigarette, tapped it on his thumbnail and lit it. He grinned at McCreary through the smoke.

"You have been quite ill, my friend. How do you feel now?"

McCreary shrugged.

"I wouldn't be knowing yet. I'm just out of bed."

"You are feeling weak?"

"How else?"

Captain Nasa smiled and clicked his tongue and took another puff at his cigarette.

"You will feel better tomorrow."

"I hope so," said McCreary without conviction.

"Then I shall call for you at midday and escort you to the airport."

McCreary slewed round and faced him squarely.

"You're in a hurry to get rid of me, aren't you?"

"The extradition order has been in force for some days," said Nasa smoothly. "I am charged to execute it as soon as possible. Meantime"—he looked down at the backs of his small brown hands—"meantime, I should prefer you

3

did not leave the hotel. It is unwise for a European to move about the city when his papers are not in order."

"I'm sure it is," said McCreary.

"Midday tomorrow then?"

"I'll be waiting for you."

"Good day, Mr. McCreary."

"The back of me hand to you, Captain!" said McCreary softly.

Nasa bowed again and went out, walking lightly, like a dancer, on the balls of his feet. McCreary waited until the door closed on him, then he cursed, fluently and foully. Nasa was a policeman, the representative of law and order—but the law worked strangely and deviously in this sprawling, gimcrack republic of three thousand islands and seventy-nine million souls. It worked better if you oiled the wheels a little. But McCreary's sole possessions were a plane ticket to Singapore, a month's salary in Indonesian rupiahs—and the luck of the Irish.

The plane ticket would lift him off one beach onto another. The rupiahs would drop 20 percent once the exchange sharks took their cut. And the luck of the Irish seemed to have run out.

McCreary put on his coat, walked down to the lounge and ordered a gin sling and a copy of the *Strait Times*. He thought it was time he started to look for a job in Singapore.

Even before he opened the paper he knew he was wasting his time. Singapore, Saigon, Bangkok, Hong Kong—entrepôt ports, hucksters' towns. There was nothing for him there.

There was nothing for him anywhere, except where the big steel skeletons reared themselves up into the sky and the rasping bits drove down through subsoil and rock into the black sands at the guts of the earth. He was an oil man, not a clerk or a merchant. He was a driller and his place was here, in the Islands, or in the Americas, or in New Guinea, or out on the fringe of the Australian desert.

But oil was a tricky business—political business. The big companies depended for their concessions on the favour of foreign governments and the expensive cooperation of local officials. They were apt to fight shy of a man who couldn't keep his fists in his pockets and his tongue between his teeth. After the business at Pakanbaru, his name would be on the blacklist, and he would have to turn to one of the smaller companies wildcatting in the marginal territories— provided he could get there.

He gave up reading the advertisements and turned to a half-page feature on the new fan dancer who had just opened a season at the Golden Dragon. But even a Eurasian fan dancer was no match for the drinks and the soggy air and the droning of the ventilators. The print danced in front of his eyes and the lush prose of the Singapore columnist made no sense at all.

Then a voice spoke to him, an English voice, but high and thin like the squeak of a bat.

"Are you McCreary?"

He looked up, startled, and saw a squat, stocky man in a tussah suit. His hair was black, his eyes were grey-green, his nose was a predatory beak and his mouth was small and red as a woman's above the square chin. His face was dead white, except where the razor stubble showed on his jawline. His hands were short and stubby and covered with thick black hair. It was hard to match him with the thin, reedy voice. McCreary looked at him a moment before he answered.

"I'm McCreary. Who are you?"

"Rubensohn. Mind if I sit down?"

"Go ahead."

He sat down and mopped his face and hands with a silk handkerchief. He took out a case of fat cigars and offered one to McCreary.

"No, thanks. I use cigarettes."

Rubensohn put the case back in his pocket. He laid his

thick hands, palms down, on the table, pushed himself back in his chair and smiled at McCreary.

"I hear you're in trouble, my friend."

"You do now?" asked McCreary mildly. "What did you hear—and where?"

"You were drilling with Palmex in Pakanbaru. You beat up a Sundanese boy, who then reported you to the police. The company disclaimed all responsibility and the police took out a warrant for your extradition. You have been sick for three days. You are to leave Djakarta on the two o'clock Garuda flight tomorrow. Is that right?"

"That's part of the story."

"What's the rest of it?"

"If it's any business of yours," said McCreary in his soft Kerry brogue, "he wrecked a new bit and thirty feet of casing, through sheer bloody carelessness. He set our operations back more than a month. I'd warned him a dozen times before. This time I hit him."

"An expensive indulgence."

"So, it's my expense. Why should you worry?"

"I don't worry, Mr. McCreary. I'm interested."

"Why?"

"I'd like to offer you a job."

McCreary stared at him blankly. "I don't understand."

"Are you interested?"

"Sure I'm interested. But what sort of a job? Where?"

"Let's have a drink, shall we?" said Rubensohn in his high, piping voice.

He clapped his hands and a Malay boy in a cockscomb headdress and a batik sarong hurried over to take the order. While they waited for the drinks, McCreary smoked a cigarette and Rubensohn watched him with ironic amusement.

Abruptly he asked: "How old are you, McCreary?"

"Thirty-eight."

"Married?"

"No."

"Any vices?"

"The usual ones."

"And an uncertain temper?"

"I don't get on with fools. I don't like careless work."

Rubensohn nodded agreement.

"Put that on the credit side. Now tell me, what's your ambition?"

McCreary grinned at him through the drift of cigarette smoke.

"Now, that's the damnedest question I've ever had put to me."

"Haven't you any ambition?"

"Sure I have, but I doubt you'd understand it if I told you."

"Try me."

McCreary's eyes clouded. With a sudden gesture he stubbed out his cigarette and leaned forward across the table.

"I don't know who you are, Rubensohn, or what you want. I don't know, and I don't much care whether you'll like the answer I give. But here it is. I'm a damn-fool Irishman with itchy feet and his home on his back. My only real talent is plugging holes in the ground to get oil. My only real ambition is to make enough money to buy me a nice little stud farm twenty miles from Dublin and see if I can breed the winner of the Grand National. Now, if you want to laugh, go ahead!"

"I'm not laughing," said Rubensohn. "So you're interested in money?"

McCreary shrugged and said, "Who isn't?"

Then the boy came back with the drinks. Rubensohn paid him and waited till he was out of earshot. He raised his glass.

"Good luck, McCreary!"

"*Slainte!*"

7

Rubensohn sipped his drink and wiped his red lips. He said, deliberately, "Money is the least important thing in the world."

"When you have it," said McCreary flatly.

"Exactly. When you have it, you know what it really is: a bundle of soiled paper, a handful of base metal, a grubby token of something far more important—credit. Myself, for instance"—he tapped his barrel chest—"I never carry more money than is necessary for the expenses of the moment. Yet I have credit everywhere . . . Hong Kong, Djakarta, New York, Paris, London."

"Lucky fellow!" said McCreary dryly.

Rubensohn ignored the interruption and went on: "With that credit, I can do business all over the world—as, in fact, I do. I can make fifty thousand pounds by lifting a telephone. I can speculate on rubber in Singapore and pepper in the Celebes. I can send Palmex shares down three points in an afternoon. And I can send your shares rocketing in the same way."

"I don't own any shares," said McCreary.

"You can," said Rubensohn in his reedy, incongruous voice, "if you accept the job."

"What is it?"

Rubensohn smiled and shook his head.

"Not here, McCreary. People talk. Other people listen. The best business is private. Look, you are, on your own showing, a man with itchy feet, who carries his home on his back. I offer you three thousand American dollars to make a trip with me to look at the job. If you don't like it, you pull out with a profit. If you want it, you keep your money and make more—lots more. What do you say?"

"Where do we go?"

"A long way from here. Out to the Celebes."

"That's still part of the Indonesian Republic. I'm under an extradition order. The police have impounded my passport. I can't get it back till I'm on the plane tomorrow."

Rubensohn smiled gently and fished in his breast pocket. He took out a small book with the symbol of the Republic of Eire on the cover and laid it on the table between them. McCreary goggled at it.

"That's my passport! How the hell did you . . . ?"

Rubensohn waved a deprecating hand.

"Credit, my dear fellow! It is useful at all levels. Captain Nasa understands that. He is much less interested in you than in a sudden increase in his bank account. He is prepared to agree to another form of transport for you, and not ask too many questions about your destination."

"And so?"

"If you agree, you will sail with me on the midnight tide."

McCreary stared at him with puzzled, brooding eyes. He shook his head.

"I don't get it, Rubensohn. I don't understand a single damn word of it. You're a businessman. You want profit. You don't give charity. Why me? I'm a driller, out of a job. How can you hope to make a profit on me?"

"At this moment," said Rubensohn slowly, "I need a man to handle certain business for me in the eastern part of the Republic. I need him urgently. I had a man lined up in Singapore. Now he can't come. You are available and I am prepared to gamble on you. The only question is: Are you prepared to gamble on me?"

"For three thousand American dollars?"

"And the prospect of much more."

McCreary looked at him a moment, then his lean face broke into a lopsided grin.

"One of us is a damn fool, Rubensohn. I've got the feeling it's me."

"Why not call it the luck of the Irish?"

McCreary shrugged and held out his hand.

"Why not indeed? All right, Rubensohn, you've got yourself a man."

Rubensohn's handclasp was slack and flabby, but his grey-green eyes were sharp with interest. He said curtly, "Good. We'll call it settled. Now, let's go to my room and talk business."

They stood up.

McCreary, moved by an odd Celtic quirk, looked at his watch. It was four-thirty. The date was the tenth of July. If there were omens in that, he had no wit to read them. And there were no prophets on hand to cry *"Cave"* to the voyager. He walked out of the room side by side with Rubensohn.

Rubensohn's room was a large, cool chamber furnished with carved teak. French windows opened onto a latticed balcony and the walls were hung with canvases by Javanese artists—misty mountain peaks, paddy fields bright with the passage of people, long beaches, gold between the hills and the iridescent sea.

But the pictures were pale and lifeless beside the girl.

She was small, high-breasted, perfect as a wax doll. Her hair was jet black. Her skin had the warm honey colour of the *métis*—the exotic bloom that flowers out of the grafting of East and West. Her body was sheathed in a dress of jade-green brocade, high to the neck. There were jewels on her fingers—diamonds and a blood-red ruby. Her feet were bare in high-heeled, open-work sandals made by a Chinese craftsman.

When they came in, she was preening herself at the mirror. She turned and looked at them curiously but said nothing. McCreary grinned at her, but there was no flicker of interest in her dark eyes. Rubensohn made a perfunctory introduction.

"This is Lisette. Lisette—a new colleague, McCreary. He will be travelling with us."

"A pleasure, ma'am," said McCreary with a flourish.

The girl said nothing. Rubensohn smiled thinly. McCreary felt faintly ridiculous.

10

Rubensohn jerked his thumb towards the French windows.

"Outside, Lisette. Wait for us."

The girl shrugged and turned away from the mirror. She walked to the French windows and opened them. McCreary saw a chaise longue set under the trailing greenery of the lattice. The girl went out, closing the door behind her.

"She's beautiful," said McCreary.

"She's mine," said Rubensohn, without emphasis. "I like decorative women."

"You're lucky to be able to afford 'em."

Rubensohn shrugged indifferently and walked across to a cabinet, unlocked the drawer and took out a small pigskin briefcase. He opened it and took out a long tube of transparent paper, which he spread carefully on the top of the table.

"Take a look at this, McCreary."

McCreary bent over the drawing. He whistled soundlessly. It was a survey chart made by a famous American company of geological surveyors. The signature was that of their best man. Both were familiar to McCreary. Rubensohn watched him shrewdly.

"Can you read it?"

"Sure, I can read it."

"What is it?"

"An oil survey."

"What does it tell you?"

"If it's genuine . . ."

"It's genuine. It cost me twenty thousand dollars."

"Cheap at the price," said McCreary. "I smell oil. Lots of it."

Rubensohn's stubby finger thrust at a point on the map.

"How long would it take you to bring in a well there?"

"Hold it a minute, Rubensohn!" McCreary straight-

11

ened up and faced him. "Let's get a few things clear. A survey's one thing. To bring in a well is something else entirely."

"How so?"

"A surveyor," said McCreary easily, "is a man, not a mole. He lives on top of the ground. He can't see underneath it. Given science and skill, he can tell you a lot about earth and rock formations. He can plot you, as this fellow's done, a promising anticline, where by rights there should be oil. But he can't tell you whether the oil's there or not. There's a gamble—a financier's gamble, a driller's gamble."

Rubensohn nodded. The answer seemed to please him. He put another question.

"I'm prepared to take the gamble. But I'd still like an answer to my question. Suppose there is oil on the anticline. At the depth shown on this survey, how long would you take to bring it in?"

McCreary considered the question.

"Is the ground cleared?"

"Yes."

"What's your equipment like?"

"The best."

"Then I'd say anything from a week to a fortnight to get the rigs up and spud in. Then another month. If this fellow's right, we strike the sand anywhere between a thousand and fifteen hundred feet. Give us six weeks in all and we should have the answer for you—good or bad."

"Good!" The word came out in a long exhalation of relief.

McCreary looked at him sharply.

"Understand it, Rubensohn! I can't make promises. I can't provide against human error and acts of God."

"I don't expect you to do that. What sort of labour force do you need?"

"An engineer first—a man who can keep my plant in

12

order and do tool dressing and machine-shop repairs. The rest I can handle with local labour, provided I have a free hand."

"I've got an engineer. Where we are going you'll have the labour—and the free hand."

"Where are we going?"

Rubensohn smiled and shook his head.

"Sealed orders, McCreary, until we're three days clear of Djakarta."

McCreary made a small gesture of indifference.

"It's all one to me, Rubensohn. You pay the piper. You name the song. But there's one thing."

"Yes?"

"Once we start work, I'm in command. I know my job and I don't like interference. Is that clear?"

"Perfectly."

Rubensohn rolled up the chart, put it back in the briefcase and locked them once more in the cabinet. He turned back to McCreary. His eyes were bright with satisfaction and his red mouth was smiling blandly.

"I like you, McCreary. I think we should go a long way together."

McCreary thrust his hands into his pockets and leaned back against the table. He said softly, "Before we go anywhere, Rubensohn . . ."

"Yes?"

"I'd like to know how much I'm getting paid, apart from the retainer."

Without a moment's hesitation Rubensohn laid down the terms.

"Three thousand dollars retainer, three hundred a week during the drilling period, a bonus of ten thousand if you bring me in a well, or the equivalent in shares in any company we form. All expenses paid during your employment and a free passage to any port in the world at the end of it. Unless, of course, you decide you'd like to continue working for me. How does that sound?"

"Fine," said McCreary coolly.

"Do you want it in writing?"

McCreary shook his head. "I'll take your word for it."

Rubensohn looked at him oddly and frowned.

"Never take any man's word about money, McCreary."

McCreary stuck a cigarette in the corner of his mouth. He grinned at Rubensohn through the first spirals of smoke.

"If a man's word is no good, his signature's no good either. But, if you want to write me a contract, do it by all means. The girl can witness it."

"I'd prefer it that way," said Rubensohn evenly. "Call her in, McCreary, and have her fix us a drink. And, McCreary . . . ?" Halfway to the French windows McCreary turned back. Rubensohn was smiling at him, but his eyes were as hard as pebbles. "Lisette is mine. Remember that, won't you?"

"With all that money," said McCreary gently, "why should you worry?"

He threw open the casement and stood looking down at the girl. She was like a bird, he thought, a bright gold-green bird under the trailing vines.

# Chapter Two

At eight o'clock the same evening, McCreary packed his canvas bag, paid his bill at the desk and walked out into the warm darkness.

The stars hung low in a velvet sky and the lights of the city were spread below him—ten miles of them, bright round the new city, intermittent in the bungalow district, where the homes of rich Chinese retreated behind the lush greenery, yellow and flaring in the kampongs, sparse and winking in the fish traps beyond the harbour of Tanjung Periuk.

He could smell the city, too, even here, on the high ground far from the fever flats and the canals of the old town where the brown people swarmed and chaffered and poured their refuse into the sluggish canals. It was a strange, exotic smell compounded of spices and rotting vegetation and drying fish and swamp water and the exhalation of two million bodies sweating in the languid air. It crept into the nostrils and cloyed the palate and clung to the clothes. You could never shake it off. And, when you went away, it remained a disturbing memory, calling you back.

McCreary put down his bag and stood a moment

against the bole of a big banyan tree to light a cigarette. Before he had doused the flame of his lighter, three betjaks pedalled up to him ringing their bells furiously. The drivers leapt out and began tugging at his sleeves, crying in parrot-like Malay about the speed and cleanliness of their vehicles. McCreary grinned and shoved them away and hefted his bag onto the seat of the first arrival. The driver laughed and mocked his rivals with a dirty word and a dirtier gesture, and the next minute they were racing down the road with plumes tossing and bells ringing and the air humming in the rubber bands stretched under the seat.

In the new town the traffic was light and McCreary leaned back in his seat and let the wind blow in his face. The driver's skinny legs threshed up and down on the pedals, and he sang and shouted and chuckled and rang his bell at every intersection and every passing car.

They were an odd people, thought McCreary, odd like the Irish. They were simple, courteous, lovers of colour and music. They walked like ballet dancers and talked like poets. But there was always the little yeast of madness fermenting under their brown skulls, and they were as apt as the Irish to run crazy with liquor or love or the simplest frustrations of living. "Amok," they called it—and when a man went amok with a hatchet or a swinging kris, he was killed quickly in a dark corner or in a police cell, because there was no hope for him anymore.

When they came to the old town, their progress was checked.

The houses of the old Dutch colonists were set back among the trees, but now four Javanese families slept in every room and their gardens were cluttered with atap huts from which the life spilled out onto the narrow streets—scuffling children, the spread baskets of the vendors, pecking chickens and peddlers with their baskets of bean curd and cooked rice and dried fish and pungent spices.

Rolls of batik were spread under matting shelters. A

16

wood-carver squatted among his carved birds and his tiny, high-breasted girls. From an open doorway came the tinkle of gamelan music, and inside McCreary could see the grotesque puppets of a shadow show above the heads of the squatting audience.

The driver swerved and pounded his bell and kicked out at the skittering children, and ten minutes later they broke into the clear space round the harbour of Tanjung Periuk. McCreary paid off the betjak and walked down to the quayside to stand looking out across the oily water of the basin.

Here were the ships of all the world: tankers from Balikpapan, rusty coasters from the China Sea, a big white Italian with her ports ablaze, homing from Sydney with the summer tourists, high-tailed junks with winking eyes on their forepeaks, a rakish merchantman from Yokohama, and the small, trim packets of the new Republican fleet, with the Garuda bird spread-eagled over their nameplates.

There was the splay of lights and the rattle of hawsers and the cough of the big dredge chewing up silt from the channel. There was the flurry of a police launch and the slow homing of a fisherman's prau and the bump of lighters against the plates of a new arrival.

Then he saw what he was looking for.

She was moored at one of the oiling berths, two hundred yards away on the eastern curve of the harbour—a long white hull with the lines of a corvette, which she probably was. She was lit from stem to stern, and he could see the hurrying figures of the Malays tending the black hoses that ran into her fuel bunkers.

He read the name on her bows—*Corsair*, Panama. He picked up his bag and walked swiftly along the quay.

A Malay serang waved him up the gangway and, when he reached the top, a young deck officer saluted him smartly and inquired his business in passable English.

"I'm McCreary."

"You are expected, sir. I understand you sail with us. Arturo Caracciolo, Second Officer."

"Happy to know you, Arturo. Where's Mr. Rubensohn?"

"In the saloon, sir. He is waiting dinner for you."

"Kind of him. Where do I go?"

"This way, sir."

He picked up McCreary's bag and led him down the companionway. McCreary noticed that the bulkheads were freshly painted and that the passage was floored with new rubber. Arturo threw open the door of a cabin and stood aside to let him enter. McCreary whistled with surprise. The cabin was as large as a stateroom. There was a bed and a writing desk and an easy chair clamped to the floor. There were bright Italian watercolours on the wall and a modern spread on the bed and drapes at the portholes. There was a small shower recess and a spacious hanging cupboard.

"Well now!" said McCreary softly. "It promises to be a pleasant trip."

Arturo smiled with boyish satisfaction.

"She was built in England, sir, and converted in Genoa. We are very proud of her."

McCreary looked at him. A nice lad. Fresh out of officers' school by the look of him. He asked, innocently, "Who is 'we'?"

"The personnel, sir. Dutch captain. Italian officers."

"And the crew?"

"Malay deckhands. Lascars in the engine room. Chinese in the galley."

McCreary nodded. He thought Rubensohn was a shrewd fellow with an eye to detail. Divide and rule. There was small room for trouble with a crew like that. He tossed his bag on the bed and went into the recess to straighten himself for dinner. Then Arturo led him to the saloon and announced him with a flourish.

"Captain Janzoon, Mr. Rubensohn. . . . Mr. Mc-Creary."

They stood to welcome him—a blond giant of a man with a cropped skull and a spade beard, Rubensohn himself and the girl.

Rubensohn greeted him with studied warmth. The girl gave him a distant nod. Captain Janzoon crushed his hand in a fist as big as a ham, slapped his shoulder and chuckled in his thick, asthmatic English.

"McCreary, eh? The wild Irish. That makes us a League of Nations. Dutch, Italian, English and a beautiful woman who is . . ."

Rubensohn's thin voice cut across the monologue. "A drink for McCreary, Captain."

Janzoon flushed but said nothing. He poured two fingers of whisky into a glass and handed it to McCreary, who tempered it carefully with water and toasted them. Janzoon and Rubensohn drank with him. The girl smoked a brown cigarette in a long holder with a gold mouthpiece and a jade tip.

Then Rubensohn put down his glass and said brusquely, "Something to remember, McCreary."

"Yes?"

"The four of us here are the only persons concerned in this . . . this enterprise. The rest are employed to run the ship and mind their own business. Is that clear?"

"Clear as me own conscience," said McCreary. "Anything else?"

"For the present, no. Do you like my ship?"

"I like it fine, the little I've seen of it. I think I'm going to enjoy myself."

"Twenty knots," said Janzoon in his thick voice. "Three thousand sea miles in her tanks. You should see my bridge. The latest! The best!"

"I always buy the best," said Rubensohn.

"We're fortunate in our boss"—McCreary grinned—"all of us."

For the first time a flicker of interest showed in Lisette's dark eyes, but McCreary did not see it. At that moment a Chinese steward came in. Janzoon spoke to him in Cantonese. When he went out, they heard him beating his little brass gong up and down the companionways and along the open deck.

Rubensohn looked at his watch and said briskly, "Dinner in fifteen minutes, gentlemen. Excuse us. Come, Lisette!"

He turned away and walked out of the saloon. The girl followed him without a word, without a glance at McCreary or Janzoon. They watched her go with speculative eyes. If there was coquetry in her walk, they did not see it. She was beautiful and cold as a wax doll.

McCreary and Janzoon looked at each other. McCreary grinned and Janzoon gave his throaty chuckle.

"What do you think of her, eh, McCreary?"

"I mustn't," said McCreary. "The stewards have warned me off the course."

Janzoon gave him a quick, shrewd glance from under his bushy brows.

"Wise fellow. We should get to know each other, you and I. I think we could be good friends."

"I'm sure we could."

Janzoon splashed more whisky into their glasses. He handed the drink to McCreary and asked casually, "Have you known Rubensohn long?"

"Four—five hours. Why?"

"He speaks highly of you."

"Nice of him."

"What do you know about him?"

"Not a thing that he hasn't told me himself.

Janzoon tossed off his drink at a gulp and wiped his lips

20

with the back of his hand. He said bluntly, "You've got a lot to learn, my friend."

McCreary smiled comfortably and said in his gentle brogue, "I learn easily. Especially when I'm paid for it."

"He's a big man," said Janzoon deliberately. "He knows what he wants and goes after it. He has great wealth. His name opens doors in Rome and Paris and Geneva and New York. This ship—he bought her from the wreckers for thirty thousand pounds and spent another fifty thousand to make her what she is today. He thinks big. He does not stint money on a project. He pays well for good service."

"What's his real business?" asked McCreary cautiously.

Janzoon shrugged.

"A man like that is interested in anything that makes profit, anywhere in the world. Today it is oil. Tomorrow it may be guns or gold or cotton. He plays the market. He floats a new company here, buys an old one there. He has the golden touch."

"Have you been with him long?"

"Ever since the *Corsair* was commissioned, three years ago. Before that I ran tankers for Bataafsche Petroleum. This is the best berth I've ever had. Good pay and better pickings."

McCreary eyed him quizzically.

"Some of the gold rubs off, eh?"

"Sometimes."

"It's a promising thought."

"For the right man," said Janzoon softly, "more than promising: a certainty."

McCreary grinned and buried his nose in his drink. Janzoon was fishing for something, but he was damned if he'd rise to the lure. A man can feel the hooks in his mouth once too often. He'd do his job, collect his money and head for home, and to hell with this blond buccaneer with the big bell laugh and the cold, calculating eyes.

Then it occurred to him that he hadn't a home, only

the vague dream of a grey stone house and a spread of green pastures where the stallions kicked up their heels, while himself in hacking jacket and wide breeches walked like a proper horse-breeding man and talked softly with the trainer and the strappers.

The humour of it took him by surprise and he laughed suddenly and gagged on his whisky, while Janzoon looked at him with puzzled hostility.

"I have said something amusing, yes?"

"Nothing! Nothing at all," said McCreary, as he mopped his mouth and his shirtfront. "A small private joke, with no malice in it."

Janzoon shook his head and clucked his disapproval.

"A thing to remember, my friend. Mr. Rubensohn doesn't appreciate jokes, especially jokes he doesn't understand."

"Then I'm sorry for the fellow," said McCreary. "It's a sad life that has no laughter in it."

"A better life than yours or mine," said Janzoon sourly, "with money and a woman like that, and the power to break a dozen men in as many minutes."

"If he doesn't enjoy it, what's the point?" McCreary shrugged and stuck a cigarette in the corner of his mouth.

Janzoon leaned forward with a lighter. He was still puzzled, but there was admiration in his eyes, a reluctant respect for this lean fellow with the lopsided grin. He said soberly:

"I like a man who can laugh at someone bigger than himself. But take a word of advice. Never laugh at Rubensohn. Never cross him in front of his woman. He's a big man, sure, but he has to feel big all the time. You watch him at dinner. Watch him any time where there is company. He must have the spotlight, the center of the stage."

McCreary shrugged and drew on his cigarette.

"So far as I'm concerned, he's welcome to it. But thanks for the advice."

Janzoon made an expansive gesture of deprecation. "Don't thank me, McCreary. I only try to help. Like I told you, I think we should be friends—good friends. Now let's go to dinner. That's another thing to remember. Rubensohn likes punctuality."

McCreary looked round in puzzlement. The table was laid in the saloon and a Chinese steward was standing in the doorway that led to the galley.

"I thought we were dining here."

"Oh, no, my friend!" Janzoon chuckled again and steered him out the opposite door. "That is for the officers. We—we are the guests of the great man. We dine in his suite, with the beautiful Lisette for company."

"Who is she?"

The question was out before he knew it, and Janzoon gave him a swift, sidelong glance that belied his indifferent answer.

"Lisette? A *métis* from Saigon, by her skin and her accent. But whether she comes from the palace or the gutter, who knows? What she is now, Rubensohn has made her. She is his product and his property."

"So he told me," said McCreary softly. "I wonder if the girl thinks the same way."

Janzoon stopped dead in his tracks. He caught McCreary's arm and swung him round, hard against the steel bulkhead. His spade beard thrust forward into McCreary's face. His voice was an angry whisper.

"Listen to me, Irishman! There are ten million beautiful women from Djakarta to Dili. All of them you can have with my blessing. But this one you don't touch. She belongs to the big man. She keeps him happy. So long as he's happy, we all stay comfortable and get rich. Make so much as a smile at her and you have two knives at your throat—his and mine! Understand?"

McCreary's smile was as bland as a babe's, his brogue as soft as butter.

"Sure, I understand. But why should I give a tinker's damn for a cold one like that? I'm a warm-hearted fellow myself and I like a smile and maybe a gentle word or two at bedtime."

"So long as you understand," Janzoon grunted sourly, and slackened his grip on McCreary's arm.

McCreary faced him squarely. His mouth was still puckered in that lopsided grin, but his eyes were bright with anger. He said bleakly, "A word in your own ear, Captain."

"Yes?"

"Keep your hands in your pockets in future. The next time you touch me like that I'll break your bloody neck!"

Janzoon's mouth dropped open with the shock of it, then without a word, he turned on his heel and led the way to Rubensohn's stateroom.

When they entered, they saw Lisette sitting languidly on a settee under a flaring nude by d'Arezzo. Her small, perfect body was sheathed in cloth of silver and her ornaments were of jade and emerald. She was smoking a cigarette and flipping idly through the pages of a French fashion magazine. She looked up when they entered, murmured a greeting and then turned back to her magazine.

We might be the milkmen, thought McCreary sourly, or the garbage collectors or the men to mend the drains. But give me half an hour under the stars and I'll teach you different, dark one.

Then he remembered the warnings he had had and he turned his attention to Rubensohn.

He was dressed meticulously as if it were the Captain's Dinner on the Pacific run, yet the first impression was of a squat frog compressed into the trappings of a gentleman. His face was whiter still, now that it had been shaved and pomaded, and the small mouth was cherry red under the jutting nose. He greeted them briskly.

"Sit down, gentlemen. We have a few minutes before our next guest arrives. I have things to say to you before he comes."

Janzoon looked up in surprise. It was clear that he, at least, was expecting no more visitors before sailing time.

He said sharply, "No more trouble, I hope."

Rubensohn looked at him with cool contempt.

"Trouble, Captain? Why should there be trouble? We sail at midnight. Our papers are cleared, our pilot is booked. Unless, of course, there is something you have forgotten?"

"No, no! Nothing! An unfortunate remark. Please forget it."

Janzoon blushed and mopped his face with his handkerchief.

Rubensohn smiled grimly at his discomfort. Then he said, "Our next guest is a friend of Mr. McCreary."

"The devil he is! What's his name?"

"Captain Nasa."

McCreary almost leapt from his chair.

"Nasa! Now look, Rubensohn, if this is some sort of a joke . . ."

"No joke at all, I assure you, Mr. McCreary." Rubensohn waved a deprecating hand. "A simple business transaction. Captain Nasa comes to be paid for services rendered."

"It's your ship, of course," said McCreary, without enthusiasm. "If it was mine, I'd not have that little bastard within a mile of it. I'd pay him his money in a dark corner and give him a kick in the teeth for good measure."

"And then have your own teeth kicked out in a Djakarta jail?" Rubensohn smiled contemptuously. "Believe me, McCreary, my methods pay better."

McCreary grinned easily and spread his hands in defeat.

"Oh, I believe you. You've got the money to prove it."

"Good!" said Rubensohn briskly. "Now we get down to business. Captain Nasa comes to be paid. Unfortunately . . ." He looked down at the backs of his short, hairy hands. ". . . Unfortunately, he now demands more money than we agreed. More money than I am prepared to pay. So I must talk to him privately. We will make a leisurely meal. Then, after the coffee, you, Captain, will have your business on the bridge. You, McCreary, will take Lisette and entertain her a little, in the saloon on the deck. When I have finished my business with Captain Nasa, I shall send for you. Is that clear?"

"It sounds like a pleasant evening," said McCreary.

"Let's hope so, for your sake," said Rubensohn dryly.

McCreary looked up sharply.

"And what does that mean?"

Rubensohn shrugged and smiled humourlessly.

"Unless I can come to terms with Captain Nasa, you, McCreary, are on the beach again."

"Would you like me to throw him in the harbour for you?" asked McCreary, with grim irony.

"Later, perhaps. For the present, you will look after Lisette and leave Captain Nasa to me."

"Like I said, it'll be a pleasure!"

He turned and made an ironic, sweeping bow to Lisette. But she did not lift her head to look at him. She was still flipping over the big shiny pages where all the women had faces like her own, cold and beautiful and dead.

Five minutes later Captain Nasa came in and they all sat down to dinner.

It was an uneasy meal. The little Javanese was cagey and suspicious, parrying the simplest questions with a sidelong smile and click of his tongue. Janzoon was clearly unhappy. He was a Dutch captain in a country where his people had once been masters but where, now, they were treated with contemptuous sufferance and sometimes with open violence. He had a hundred thousand pounds of ship under his command and he would not be happy until he had cleared the channel lights and was well away outside the territorial limit.

Lisette made no contribution at all to the conversation, and McCreary was plagued with the Celtic temptation to bait the little policeman, who sat there grinning and clucking his contempt of the Westerners who had to pay him for the simplest service.

Only Rubensohn was completely master of himself and of the situation. He led them like a chamber group through the courtesies of the meal. His thin, reedy voice flattered and cajoled and admonished and tossed topic after topic round the table, so that, out of the hostility and conflict, there came a kind of harmony, illusory and temporary, but enough to last them to the coffee and the first brandy.

Then, without emphasis, Rubensohn dismissed them.

"If you will excuse us a while, Lisette, gentlemen, Captain Nasa and I have business to discuss."

They filed out of the stateroom and closed the door behind them. Janzoon left them without a word, and McCreary and the girl walked up the companionway to the afterdeck.

The air was warm and heavy with the smell of the city and the jungle, but Lisette shivered when McCreary linked his arm in hers. As he led her over to the railing, her sandals made a small dry clatter on the steel plates of the deck. They stood together, leaning over the rail and watching the play of lights on the slack, oily water. McCreary felt the skin of her arm, silken under his touch, but there was no pulse to it, no answer to the tentative pressure of his fingers.

He said gently, "Are you cold, dark one?"

"No. I'm quite warm, thank you."

Her voice had the upward, questioning lilt of the *métis*, but there was no life there either. It was like the tinkle of the little glass bells that fluttered outside the shrines of the old gods. McCreary wondered how it would sound when she laughed and how long it was since she had been touched to passion or to tears.

He asked her again, in the soft honeyed brogue of the Kerryman, "We're to be together for a long time, it seems. Could you not give me a smile sometimes and a word to pass the hour of the day?"

"Why should it matter to you whether I smile or frown?"

"It'd make me feel better," said McCreary lightly. "More of a man, maybe, and less of footloose gypsy with no hearth to warm his toes at and no wife to warm his bed."

"I'm paid to do that for one man now. Two would be too much."

She said it simply, inconsequently, staring out across the water to the banked lights of a passing tanker.

"There's no question of payment," said McCreary with a grin. "I'm as poor as a village fiddler. So what I get I must get for love, and what I give is out of a full heart and an empty pocket. So I'm out of the market. Is that any reason why you shouldn't give me the pleasure of a smile or two? Is the world such a sad place that you can't find a damn thing to laugh about? Look now . . ." He pointed out across the bay to where the tugs were hauling the big white Italian ship, snout first, into the channel. "There's a sight for you. You know where she's going? Singapore first and then Colombo and afterwards Naples. . . ."

"I've been to Naples." Her voice was empty of interest.

"You have now? And you stayed no doubt in a fine hotel down on the waterfront in the best suite that Rubensohn's money could buy."

"I did."

"And you had every damn waiter in the place tripping over himself to give you service, and every damn huckster trying to sell you something."

28

"I did."

"Where else have you been now?"

She shrugged lightly and counted off the names: "Oh, many places—New York, London, Paris, Cannes, Madrid, Vienna."

"And every one of them was like the other, wasn't it?"

"Yes."

"Then, don't you see, dark one, you haven't lived an hour or a moment of it? You don't know what the world's about or what the taste of happiness feels like."

"Happiness?" She lingered on the word almost with scorn. "Happiness, no . . . that I do not know. But the world? I know it better than you, McCreary, much, much better."

"And how would you make that out, dark one? When I've wandered the world since I was sixteen years of age?"

"I didn't have to wander. The world came to me."

"Why shouldn't it? And you with all that dark and secret beauty."

She did not bridle at the compliment as another woman might have done. Her hand lay slack and unresponsive in his own. She said baldly, "In the Peacock Pavilion there were no secrets. All the doors opened to a man who had money."

"Where was this?" McCreary's voice came dry and harsh.

"Saigon."

"How did you get there? Is that where Rubensohn found you?"

"Yes. I had the talent to please him, it seemed, and he is a difficult man to please. More than that, it gives him satisfaction to present me to respectable people, to have men bow over my hand and women admire my clothes and jewels, and to know all the time that I am a woman he has picked out of the gutter in Saigon."

"And you?"

"Me?" Again he heard in her voice the brittle music of the old and ugly gods. "I am content. Why should I be otherwise? There are two hundred women in the Peacock Pavilion. Here I am only one. And better paid than any of the others."

"Until Rubensohn gets tired of you."

"Could you do better for me, McCreary?" There was no anger in her voice, only a thin, cool irony.

"I might," said McCreary soberly, "if the passion took me and took you at the same time and we could go far away to make a new beginning."

Then, for the first time, he heard her laugh. But there was no joy in it for him or her.

"You're a fool, McCreary."

"That's something I've known a long time, dark one. But I like my folly better than Rubensohn's wisdom."

"Why did you join him then?"

"Because he offered me good money to do the only job I'm trained for—drill for oil."

"Is that all?"

"What else should there be?"

"You were afraid of Captain Nasa."

Now it was McCreary's turn to laugh—a gusty bellow that rang out across the harbour and startled the homing fishermen and the sea birds roosted on the anchored beacons. Lisette drew away from him, startled.

"Afraid of him? Why should I be afraid of a teak-faced jack-in-office like that? The most he could do was to put me on the plane to Singapore. I was prepared for that. There was nothing to be afraid of. Then Rubensohn came along and made me an offer and told me he'd squared Nasa to allow me to be extradited on the *Corsair*. It wasn't even illegal, though I don't doubt Nasa made it sound a big concession and charged him plenty for it."

"Then why has Nasa come here tonight, if not for you?"

"Whatever the reason, dark one, and whatever Rubensohn says, he didn't come here for me."

"Why then?"

There was an odd note in her voice that puzzled him, but her eyes were blank as a doll's and her face as beautiful. He leaned back against the rail and laughed at her.

"Should you care why? Should I? It's Rubensohn's business and Rubensohn's money. So long as we get paid, who cares? One thing you can be sure of, Nasa's doing better than either of us—except me!"

Then he took her in his arms and kissed her and she beat at his breast with small, helpless hands, but he held her until the coldness melted out of her and her lips were warm to his own.

# Chapter Three

A long time later, it seemed, they sat together on the canvas hatch cover, McCreary smoking peacefully and Lisette repairing the damage to her lips and hair.

McCreary said softly, "So, now we know."

Her face was in shadow, so that he could not see whether she smiled or frowned, but when she answered her voice was no longer brittle, but low and strained.

"So we know—what? That you are a man who warms quickly to a woman?"

"And you a woman who can warm to me?"

"That, too. But where does it lead us?"

"Wherever you want," said McCreary. "Over the side and down the gangplank and back to the city. We can start from there."

She shook her head.

"And you with a police order against you and no money in your pocket?"

His hand reached out to her in the darkness, but she drew back from it. He challenged her brutally.

"So we stay here, me wanting you, you wanting me, me trying to keep my hands and my eyes off you, night and day, and you in another man's bed, because he's got more money than I have. Is that what you want?"

"It's not what I want, McCreary. It's what I have. I intend to keep it until someone offers me better."

"Isn't love better? Even with the risks of it?"

"Love?" The word was a tinkling mockery. "You call this love? You think you are the only man for whom I have had this feeling? You think I believe I am the only woman who has moved you? Be honest, McCreary, as I am with you."

"So, Rubensohn does own you after all."

"He owns what he has paid for, nothing more. Look, McCreary . . ." Her voice warmed suddenly and she laid her small hand on his. "In another time, in another place, there might have been hope for us. But not here, not with him. Don't you see? If he knew what has passed between us just now, he would do everything in his power to hurt and humiliate us—destroy us even."

"It'd take a bigger man than Rubensohn to do that," said McCreary.

"You think so? You don't know him as I do. He stops at nothing to get what he wants."

"I'm a determined man myself," said McCreary lightly.

"You're a bigger fool than you know, McCreary," she said.

And before he had time to deny it, a Chinese steward came padding round the deck to tell them that Rubensohn was ready for them.

The first thing they saw when they entered Rubensohn's suite was Captain Nasa slumped across the table, snoring noisily. There was a champagne bucket at his elbow and an overturned glass in front of him. A runnel of spilt liquor dripped from the table edge onto his lap. Rubensohn himself was standing over by the porthole, smoking one of his fat cigars.

Lisette stared at Nasa in amazement.

McCreary swore softly: "Mother of God! He's out to it! Drunk as a fiddler!"

Rubensohn smiled and waved his cigar expansively.

"A good Moslem never touches hard liquor. Nasa forgot his faith—and this is the result."

"Did you finish your business with him?" asked McCreary.

"Oh yes. Satisfaction on both sides. I brought out the champagne to seal the bargain. I might as well have saved it."

"It didn't take him long to get like this. We've only been gone half an hour."

Rubensohn looked at him sharply, but McCreary's eyes were innocent of malice.

"These fellows can never hold their liquor," said Rubensohn flatly. "Now he presents us with another problem: how to get him home."

"Simple enough," said McCreary airily. "Call a betjak, bundle him into it and tell the boy to take him to police headquarters."

"Not so simple as it looks, McCreary."

"Oh, why not?"

Rubensohn gestured impatiently.

"Because he was here, unknown to his superiors, for the purpose of negotiating a bribe. If we call a betjak to the ship, the driver will know where he came from. He will be questioned and so will we—and we are due to sail in an hour from now."

"He's in no condition to walk home." McCreary grinned.

"No, but he can be walked away from the ship, down to the market area. Then he can be bundled into a cab and sent on his way."

"True enough."

"Then," said Rubensohn fastidiously, "I suggest you

hoist him up and get him out of here as quickly as possible.
He has fouled the place enough already."

"Now, wait a minute!" McCreary was instantly hostile.
"Why me? Why not one of your deckhands, one of the
lascars?"

Rubensohn smiled at him blandly.

"Because, at this moment, they are all busy preparing
to put us to sea. Because they are ignorant fellows who
could not possibly explain themselves as nurses to a
drunken policeman. Because you, McCreary, are in my
debt and I ask this as a small favour. . . ." He chuckled
and went on in his high bird's voice. "And because now, at
last, you have your chance to throw him in the harbour if
you want to."

McCreary looked at him a moment, debating the
question. Then he said coolly, "That's four reasons you've
given me, Rubensohn, and the only one that holds water is
that I owe you something. For that I'll do it."

He bent over the snoring Captain Nasa and slung one
arm over his shoulder, then heaved him out of the chair by
main force. Nasa's full weight hung on him like a coal sack.

"Put his fez on, Rubensohn, and steady him while I get
my grip. I'll need a lift up the companionway."

Rubensohn clapped the black fez on Nasa's lolling head
and McCreary half walked, half dragged him to the door
like an old friend roistering home from a party.

Lisette stood aside to let him pass and watched him
stagger down the passageway and up the companion ladder,
while Rubensohn heaved and grunted to get the pair of
them safely on deck.

"Get him well away from the waterfront," said Rubensohn tersely. "If he's too much trouble, toss him in the
canal."

"I've been drunk myself," said Mike McCreary. "I
couldn't do that to my worst enemy. Come on, Nasa me

36

boyo, see if you can't walk a little and take the weight off my shoulders."

And, whistling a tuneless little jig, he staggered down the gangplank, while Captain Nasa breathed thickly and noisily down his collar.

The bunkering crew were too busy uncoupling the hoses to give them more than a passing glance, and once they were clear of the *Corsair*'s berth, the dock was almost deserted. But there was always the chance of a prowling waterside patrol, so McCreary decided to dive straight into the huddle of warehouses and work his way round by a longer detour to the fringe of the market area, where the betjaks had their stands.

At first he tried to make Nasa walk with him, but the little man's legs dangled slack as a puppet's and his polished shoes scuffed in the dust as McCreary dragged him into the shadows of the loading ramps between the warehouses. More than once he had to stop and lean against a wooden wall or a concrete pylon to take a breath and ease the weight on his shoulder. All the time his eyes and ears were alert for the coming of the dock police, and he wondered what answer he would give if they questioned him.

Finally he cleared the warehouses and found himself on a narrow path fringed with jungle growth, at the end of which he could see the shape of a bamboo bridge and the gleam of canal water and a huddle of yellow lights. To judge from the smell and the distant clatter of voices and the yapping of dogs, the night market was in full swing.

He decided it would be safe to give up all pretense of walking the captain and hoist him over his shoulder— easier, too, than dragging a dead weight as he had done for the last fifteen minutes.

In the shelter of a big banyan tree he halted and let the little captain slide to the ground. He stood a moment, to take a breath and flex his muscles and loosen his tie. He realized that his clothes were sodden with sweat and clung to his body. Then he realized something else.

Nasa wasn't snoring anymore. He wasn't breathing either.

He knelt swiftly and laid his ear to the little man's chest. He could hear no heartbeat. He felt for his pulse. There was none. The hands were cold, though the air was hot and reeking. McCreary fumbled for his lighter, snapped on the flame and held it close to Nasa's face. The eyes were open and staring. The mouth was slack and a small runnel of spittle had dried against the jaw.

By all elementary tests, Captain Nasa was dead.

Swiftly McCreary went through his pockets. In the breast pocket there was a wallet. In the fob of his trousers a handful of small notes. There was a handkerchief and a packet of American cigarettes and a cheap Japanese lighter. McCreary opened the wallet and went through it quickly. Letters, a police card, a photograph of a woman and a child, five hundred rupiahs in notes—nothing more. He wiped the wallet with his handkerchief and put it carefully back in the breast pocket. Acting on a sudden impulse, he shoved the lighter and the cigarettes into his own pocket.

Then he lifted Nasa's body by the armpits and dragged it behind the bole of the banyan tree. The fez rolled off in the process. He picked it up, dusted it carefully and cocked it over the staring eyes. Then he wiped his hands on his own handkerchief, stepped out onto the path and walked swiftly back the way he had come.

When he reached the shelter of the warehouses, he stopped, propped himself in a sheltered angle and lit a cigarette: a dead man's cigarette with a dead man's lighter. His hands were trembling and the small yellow flame wavered in front of his nose. A shiver went through him. The sweat on his body felt suddenly cold, as if the fever were coming on again. He leaned back against the slats of the wall and inhaled deeply, and battled to set his thoughts in order.

"Think about it, McCreary. Think! Think! Don't stand here like a bog-trotting idiot. A man's dead. He died in your arms. You're in a mess. Up to the neck. Nasa's dead, but a man doesn't die of half a bottle of champagne. Most men don't even get drunk on it, not snoring drunk. That's one lie chalked up to Mister goddamn Rubensohn. And here's another. Nasa came to be paid off. According to Rubensohn, he was paid off. But all he had in his pockets was spending money—not enough to pay for fixing an extradition order, not half enough to pay for whatever other services Rubensohn has had from him. Other services? But what? Big enough to make Nasa think of raising the ante. Rubensohn is in oil. Oil is a tricky business. You need friends in government quarters . . .

"A policeman doesn't have friends. But he does have power—lots of power in a gimcrack republic like this one, where squeeze and graft are the order of the day. So he raised the ante. And Rubensohn killed him. Poisoned his drink, or simply crammed the stuff down his neck at gunpoint, because it's easier for a man to die unconscious than to feel a bullet tearing into his guts. The rest is crude stage management: slop champagne over his chin and down his shirtfront and keep talking till a thick-headed Irishman like McCreary takes him off your hands. If there's any trouble, McCreary's the man. McCreary's the pea under the thimble. He killed him to get his passport back. He's got a charge of violence against him from Pakanbaru. If there's no trouble, you've got McCreary, too—to bring your well in and hand you a million on a silver plate. Clever fellow, Rubensohn . . . clever, clever fellow. And like the lady said, McCreary, you're a bigger fool than you look."

The cigarette was smoked to a stub and the stub was scorching his fingers. He dropped it in the dust and ground it out with his heel. Then he lit another. His hands were steadier now and his mind was clearer. He saw plainly the choice he must make.

He could cut loose from Rubensohn, here and now. Go back to town and take the two o'clock plane to Singapore the following day, and hope the police didn't catch up with him in the meantime. But they probably would catch up with him, and when they did they'd shove him in jail and work on him, in their aimless, pitiless Asiatic fashion, with rattan canes, until they'd killed him or beaten a confession out of him. After which they'd kill him anyway.

There was no profit in that. But there might be profit in Rubensohn. If he could command himself enough to put a grin on his face and a spring to his step, and walk back to the ship to tell Rubensohn that Nasa was still snoring his way home, Rubensohn would believe him, because he would want to believe him. And then . . . ? He would do the job he was paid for. He would watch and maneuver until one day he had Rubensohn where he wanted him, looking down the gun barrel and squealing for mercy. He would take Lisette and he would take his money, and then he would remind him of Nasa and hand him the cheap little lighter for a souvenir.

He knew it was a wild hope. He had even enough humour to laugh at it. But it would give him something to plan for and work for and—what a cross-grained Celt needed most of all—somebody to fight.

Slowly and with relish he smoked the last of his cigarette. Then he straightened his tie and smoothed his crumpled jacket and walked briskly back to the *Corsair*, whistling the march of Brian-na-Kopple, who was the greatest fighter of them all in Kerry of the Kings.

When he reached the ship, he found Rubensohn pacing the deck, with a cigar stuck in his red woman's mouth and his hands clasped behind his back in the attitude of a pensive Napoleon. McCreary fell into step beside him, and Rubensohn questioned him sharply.

"You're back quicker than I expected. Did you have any trouble with Nasa?"

"None at all." McCreary's tone was as casual as be damned. "I pushed him into a betjak and paid the driver to cart him round till he sobered up. I told him he'd get a beating if he delivered him before he was respectable."

Rubensohn spluttered over his cigar and broke into his high laughter.

"Magnificent, McCreary! Magnificent! By the time he wakes, we'll be heading out of the channel and turning our noses eastward."

"I hope we'll be a long way farther than that," said McCreary. The irony was lost on Rubensohn, who strode out faster now, head thrust forward as if butting his way towards a new conquest. He took the cigar out of his mouth and stabbed it towards the open sea.

"There are big things ahead of us, McCreary, bigger than you dream. Do you know why I am here, in this stinking backwater at the wrong end of the world? For money? I am stifled with money. From now till the day I die, I can have the best and not raise a finger to work for it. But it is not enough. A man needs more than that. He needs the challenge to himself, the urge to exercise the power that is in him. And here"—he flung out his arms in a theatrical gesture—"here in this sea of three thousand islands, is one of the few places in the world where he can still do it. The wealth of Europe was built here, by the Portuguese and the Dutch and the British. But Europe is dying now, stifled by legalism and diplomacy and the controls that men impose on themselves for an illusion of security. You know what I am, McCreary?"

"I've been trying to find a name for it," said McCreary quietly.

"Then I'll give you the name. I'm a filibuster, a privateer—the nearest thing to the old merchant princes who hired their mercenaries and primed their own guns

41

and plied the ports of the world under their own flag. The islands here, South America perhaps, are the only places in the world where a man like me can be free to breathe and build his own empire with his own brains and guts and money. Can you understand that?"

"I think so. It's a big thought. It needs time to brood on."

Rubensohn threw back his head and laughed his high, whinnying laugh.

"You'll have time, McCreary. I will show you things that beggar the thousand and one nights of Haroun al Raschid. I will show you a prince whose rivers run with jewels, who eats from gold plate and keeps five hundred women for his own pleasure. I will show you the slave routes, where the beauty of the world is brought for sale. I will show you how to multiply money like a gambler's dream . . ."

He broke off and stood a moment as if drunk with his own eloquence. The light from the bridge above fell full on his face, and when McCreary looked at it, he saw the bright, mad eyes of a visionary and the curling, cruel mouth of a caliph. The man believed every word of what he was saying, and McCreary had more than half a conviction that he should believe it too.

Then, abruptly, the mood of exaltation passed and Rubensohn was himself again, hard-eyed, canny, the man of affairs instructing his hireling.

"Bring me in a well, McCreary. Bring it in fast and you'll never regret it. There's a full rig and a full range of spares crated down in the hold. You can start work the day after we land."

"And where will that be?"

Rubensohn chuckled contemptuously and shook his head.

"Three days out, McCreary, and I'll show you on the map."

"You don't trust your staff very far, do you?" said McCreary tartly.

Rubensohn looked at him with cold irony.

"With money or a woman, trust nobody."

"Do you expect your staff to trust you?" McCreary was nettled. He was damned if he'd be put down by this putty-faced Napoleon.

Rubensohn's answer was as chill as a knife blade.

"I don't give a damn whether they trust me or not, McCreary. I expect them to give value for value received. If they don't, I take it out on their hides—now, or ten years hence. I've got a long memory. Do I make myself clear?"

"Sure," said McCreary easily, "it's clear enough. It's just that I'm new here. I like to know the rules. I don't carry a chip on my shoulder, but I don't like to feel that other people are trying to knock one off it."

Rubensohn shrugged and turned away. The discussion was closed. The subject was trivial. He had no further interest in it. McCreary bit back his anger and stood leaning against the rail, watching the last small traffic on the dock.

He saw the bunkering crew reel in their hoses and move away. He saw the small brown figures standing by the bollards, waiting to cast off. He saw the pilot come aboard, a bustling dapper little Javanese who bore an uncanny resemblance to Captain Nasa. He saw the gangway hauled inboard and the deckhands waiting with the officer of the watch.

He felt the slow shudder as the engines started, heard the shrill note of the bos'n's whistle and the thresh of water as the screw began to turn.

Then they were nosing out, slowly, tentatively, into the channel, past the dark skeletons of the fish traps, past the bobbing lights of the praus, eastward into the moonrise, towards a nameless island in a nameless sea.

The air was heavy as incense clouds, but McCreary felt

suddenly cold and naked. He thought of Captain Nasa huddled in death among the spreading roots of the banyan tree. And, when a barefoot seaman padded past him on the deck, it was as if someone were walking over his own grave.

# Chapter Four

The sky was a dazzle of blue, the sea a flat mirror, broken only by the wash of their passing. Java was far south by now, slanting downward towards the ninth parallel. To port lay a huddle of islands, blurred in the heat haze. Their names were an exotic mystery: Pulau Pulau, Kemudjan, and the high peak that heaved itself sheer from the water was called Karimunjawa. Through the glasses they could see the feathery green of the hinterland, the sliver of gold that was the beach and the tiny, bird-like shapes that were the boats of the island people.

They were thrusting eastward, dead on the sixth parallel, towards the Makassar Straits and the southern tip of the Celebes. The steady beat of the engines never faltered and their day was a bright but languid monotony. A canopy had been stretched on the afterdeck and a canvas swimming pool slung beyond it.

McCreary and Lisette spent most of the first day stretched on towels under the canopy, stripped down to swimming costumes; but Rubensohn sat in a deck chair, immaculate in silk shirt and linen slacks, as if afraid or ashamed to expose his white, slug-like skin to the sun. A Chinese steward wandered by at intervals to serve iced

45

beer, and when young Arturo came off watch, he, too, stripped down to swimming trunks and came to join the little group under the awning.

He looked with frank admiration on the lithe, perfect body of Lisette and tried at first to woo her with Latin compliments. But, when he felt Rubensohn's cold eyes on him, he flushed and lapsed into embarrassed small talk. Lisette, herself, was cool and composed, and McCreary was conscious of her secret contempt for her boyish suitor and for Rubensohn himself.

Since their brief interlude of the night before, they had had no moment of privacy or contact. Even when they swam together in the pool, Rubensohn's cold eyes followed them, and when they lay under the awning, Rubensohn dominated the talk, chopping off each theme that he could not share, capping each incident with a tale of his own. The man's boorishness irritated McCreary, but he learned quickly to control himself. He needed Rubensohn happy and unsuspicious. He needed Lisette, too, but he knew he would have to wait for time and secrecy.

Meantime, he set himself to open diplomatic relations with the Italian officers—young Arturo, with his bright, guileless eyes and his pride in his first post; Agnello, the horse-faced Florentine who ran the engines, a sad fellow, who wandered up on deck, with a piece of cotton waste in his hands and his overalls sodden with oil and sweat, to take the air; Guido, the stocky little Neapolitan with the flashing eyes and the dark Arab face.

Guido was the wireless officer, and McCreary took special pains with him, chuckling over his first dirty stories, capping them with one or two of his own. Guido had all the Neapolitan's love of salacious intrigue, and McCreary had an eye to the time when he might want a quiet look at the *Corsair's* wireless log.

With the first officer, Alfieri, he was less successful. Alfieri was a tall, saturnine Venetian who ran the ship with cool efficiency and kept his party manners for Rubensohn and Lisette. McCreary judged him an ambitious fellow who would make his way in the world without too much care for the faces he kicked on the climb up.

Janzoon, himself, was at pains to heal the breach between them. On the afternoon of the first day, he made a fumbling apology, then took McCreary up onto the bridge for a tourist's lecture on the equipment. Then he took him into his own cabin and poured him a double whisky and soda and talked shrewdly and probingly about an alliance.

"Now, I think, you begin to see how it goes here, eh?"

McCreary shrugged and smiled at him over his glass.

"I'm learning. A little here, a little there. You know?"

"Sure, I know," said Janzoon. "You learn that the big man goes his own way and doesn't give a curse for anyone else. You learn that he is jealous of his pride and of his girl. After that, what does he care?"

"Nothing, I'd say."

"Right!" said Janzoon in his thick, emphatic voice. "So you do what he pays for, and for the rest you make a little trade on the side, eh?"

McCreary made a rueful mouth.

"I've never been a very good trader, Janzoon. Otherwise I'd be richer than I am now. My great-grandfather was a Kerry horse coper, but the talent seems to have died before it reached me."

"Pfui!" Janzoon's ham fist waved aside the argument. "It takes no talent, only know-how. Look, I'll show you!"

He got up and opened the clothes locker behind McCreary's chair. From the top shelf he took half a dozen bundles of notes, which he flapped under McCreary's nose.

"You know what that is?"

"Money," said McCreary. "I can smell it."

"Paper!" said Janzoon, with rambunctious contempt. "Unless you know where to spend it. Indonesian rupiahs! They wouldn't buy you a glass of beer in Singapore. In

London you might as well use 'em to wipe your backside. But there, in the Islands, you can buy gold with 'em and jade, if you know where to look for it, and diamonds washed down from the inland rivers. And these things you can sell for good hard dollars or Swiss francs. You see how it goes?"

"Sure," said McCreary. "But I don't see why you need a partner. And besides, I've got a short-term assignment from Rubensohn. After that I'm out."

Janzoon bent forward, dropped his voice to a confidential whisper and tapped McCreary's knee with a stubby finger.

"Why else do I tell you about the market and the opportunities here, except to show you why you should stay?"

"It depends on Rubensohn, doesn't it?"

"It depends on you," said Janzoon, with throaty emphasis. "Rubensohn needs men. He wouldn't say so himself, but he does. If he sees that you play the game his way, keep your tongue still and your hands off his girl, there is nothing you cannot come to. Believe me, McCreary!"

He heaved himself up again, and this time brought out from the cupboard a chamois bag bigger than his own fist and tipped the contents out on the table. McCreary saw a medley of stones, cut and uncut, winking in the shaft of sunlight from the porthole. Janzoon lifted them in his hand and let them sift slowly back onto the table.

"Two more bags like that, McCreary, all on the one trip. A hundred percent profit made by bazaar haggling and scalping the percentage on the money market."

"Then why share it?"

Janzoon took the question in his stride, almost, thought McCreary, as if he had been briefed for it. He said earnestly:

"Because two men can make three, four times as much as one. It's a question of time, you see. I'm a ship's captain. The time I have in port for private business is half that of an ordinary officer or seaman. With someone like you, free to move, to make the contacts, we could do big business, really big."

McCreary grinned happily and poured himself another shot of the captain's whisky.

"I like the idea, Janzoon, but I don't see how I'm going to get time for trade when I'm supposed to be drilling for oil."

"The oil is for six weeks, two months, three. Afterwards is what you must think about."

"I'll do that," said McCreary genially. "I'll think about it very carefully. And thanks for the tip."

"Nothing," said Janzoon. "I help you to help myself. Down the hatch!"

"Up the Irish!"

They drank together like a pair of conspirators and McCreary walked out into the blazing sunshine of the deck, with two new thoughts buzzing in his brain. The first was that Rubensohn was trying, through Janzoon, to buy him, lock, stock and barrel, to make him a permanent member of the club. All the flash and flurry of easy money was unnatural, out of character for both men.

The second thing, and the more important, was that the oil venture was a short-term project—six weeks, two months, three. That in itself was a matter for suspicion. Oil wasn't handled like that. Oil was big business, developing business. You brought in one well, you tried to bring in others. You set about extending your holdings and opening up new areas. You thought in terms of pipelines and storage installations, of tanker contracts and harbourage and political protection and capital issues. Oil was a lifetime business, even for the wildcatters. Yet here, the talk was of bringing in a well in a couple of months, then peddling currency and stones in the bazaar ports. None of it made sense. Or did it?

He leaned on the rail and stood a long time looking

down at the hypnotic wash of foam and water against the flanks of the *Corsair*. He thought he was being paid small compliment. He was a bull-headed Irishman with the wanderlust in him and a taste for the lighter side of living and loving. But he wasn't to be bought with a few dirty notes, and he thought he could see a hole in the wall as clearly as the next man.

He thought, too, that he understood why Captain Nasa had been killed.

He tossed the stub of his cigarette over the rail and watched it whirl away in the thresh of green water and white foam.

Then he walked slowly aft to join Rubensohn and Lisette under the awning.

To his surprise he found Lisette alone. She was sitting in a striped deck chair, leafing through a magazine. Her eyes were hidden from him by modish sunglasses.

He eased himself into the chair beside her and asked quietly, "Where's Rubensohn?"

Without lifting her head from the magazine, she said flatly, "Gone to his cabin. The heat was too much for him. He said he would rest till dinnertime."

"Good. Then we can talk awhile."

"Not for long. I'm going below, too."

"Listen, dark one!" His voice was urgent and angry. "We've rehearsed this part, remember? I know the lines by heart. This is the next act . . . new scene, new time, new complications. You're in it, too, like it or not."

"I've told you before, McCreary. I'm not interested. I refuse to be involved. I've told you why."

"It's murder, sweetheart," said McCreary softly.

He might have told her the time of the day for all the reaction he got. Calmly she turned another page of the magazine and went on scanning the photographs and the captions. Her small hands were steady on the glossy paper.

She said simply, "Whatever it is, it is not my business."

50

"Listen, Lisette! Last night . . ."

"Last night was a wild moment best forgotten."

"You told me I was a fool and . . ."

"And now you've found out?" Her voice was tinkling with mockery. "Then please don't make me part of your folly. Now, McCreary, will you go or must I?"

"I'll go." He hoisted himself out of the chair and stood a moment looking down at her. His tone was harsh with disappointment and frustration. "You've had it rough, Lisette, and you're scared to lose the little you've salvaged. But you'll have it rougher yet, and you'll find that Rubensohn won't help at all, at all. He'll throw you to the sharks and watch them eat you. When that time comes, you'll remember what I'm telling you now. I want to help you. But I can't unless you help me too."

Then, for the first time, she took off her sunglasses and he saw that her eyes were somber and rebellious. She looked at him a long moment and shook her head slowly.

"Nobody can help you, McCreary. Nobody can help me either. We're both lost. The only difference between us is that I know it and you don't. Now for God's sake leave me in peace!"

He turned on his heel and left, cursing softly and fluently to himself. She watched him striding swiftly down the deck and scrambling up the companionway that led to the wireless cabin. Then the magazine slipped from her hands and she sat a long time, numb and staring, while the warmth drained out of her golden body and the chill crept in around her frightened heart.

Guido, the wireless operator, was lounging in his chair, waiting for the English bulletin from Singapore radio. When McCreary stuck his head into the cabin, he looked up, and his swarthy face broke into a grin of welcome.

"Come in, *amico!* Come in! *S'accomodi!* Make yourself at home. You like a drink?"

"I could use one, Guido." McCreary sat himself on the bunk, while Guido lifted the cap from a bottle of Pilsener and poured it foaming into a tooth glass. "You sure you're not busy?"

"Busy?" Guido made grand opera gestures and reached for another bottle of Pilsener. "Nothing important—the English news from Singapore. Then nothing till the weather reports at seven and the confirmation at eleven. Unless anybody wants to send a radio or make a telephone call to his girl."

"Not me," said McCreary, with conviction. "I've given up women. *Salute*, Guido!"

"You what?" Guido was so startled by the news that he forgot to answer the toast. His beer remained suspended halfway to his mouth. "Give up women? Impossible. Unnatural. I've tried. It can't be done. The only way I can save my strength is to come to sea. Even then I have to remind myself that I am still a man. Look!"

McCreary slewed round to admire the double row of bosomy film stars gummed to the bulkhead at the foot of the bunk.

"You like them?"

"At least they're less trouble that way," said McCreary ruefully.

"Less trouble, sure, but less pleasure, too. *Non è vero?*"

McCreary chuckled. After his passage at arms with Lisette, the comic lechery of the little Neapolitan was a refreshing change.

Guido cocked his head on one side and looked at him like a speculative parrot. He jerked a knowing thumb in the direction of the afterdeck.

"Talking about women, *amico*, this one we got here . . . What do you think, eh?"

"Cold," said McCreary, with flat conviction. "Cold as a fish. No profit to any man."

Guido nodded vigorously and rubbed his thumb and index finger together in the familiar Neopolitan gesture that says "money."

"That's the only thing that warms them, *amico*. That's why they're no good to fellows like you and me who like a little honest loving without having to pay for every kiss and every caress. There was a girl once in Reggio . . ."

"Maybe . . ." said McCreary hastily, "maybe we should catch the news from Singapore, eh?"

"Sure, sure! You like to listen too? We can take it on the speaker."

"I'd like that."

Guido flicked the switch, and after a few moments the voice of the news announcer faded in:

". . . and no further student demonstrations were reported. A late message from our correspondent in Djakarta states that Indonesian police authorities are seeking to interview a former oil company employee, Michael Aloysius McCreary, in connection with the murder of a senior official of the Djakarta police department. McCreary, who was due to be extradited for an act of violence in the Pakanbaru area, has disappeared. A continual watch is being maintained on airport and dock areas in case McCreary tries to leave the country. . . ."

McCreary reached over and flicked the switch and the announcer was cut off.

Guido looked at McCreary with bright, shrewd eyes. He said, "That's you they talk about, eh?"

"That's me, Guido."

"Killed a policeman, eh? Big stuff!" Half of Naples is bandit at heart, and Guido's eyes widened with admiration. "What happened, *amico*? Did he steal your girl? Did he . . . ?"

"I didn't kill him, Guido."

Guido patted him paternally on the shoulder.

"Whatever you say, *compar'*. Your business, not mine. You can trust Guido."

McCreary slewed round sharply to face him.

"I can? Good! Can I trust you to say nothing of this to anybody for two days?"

"Trust me? *Senz'altro!* I would swear it on the bones of my mother, if I knew who she was."

"I'll take your word for it, Guido," said McCreary, with a wry grin. "But I still didn't kill him."

He stood up and slammed one bunched fist into the palm of his other hand. He was in it now, for good and all. He'd been named to every police department in the East as the man behind the gun. Like it or not, he was a member of the Outsiders' Club. It was time he learned the rules and started playing them—hard.

# Chapter Five

On the morning of the third day, Rubensohn called McCreary to his stateroom. Captain Janzoon was there with Lisette, and Rubensohn's squat figure was bending over a chart spread on the table.

They looked up when he entered, a lean, gangling figure with his crooked grin and his bright, shrewd eyes. Rubensohn greeted him warmly enough and pointed to the chart.

"The big day, McCreary. The day of revelations. Come here and look."

The three of them bent over the chart, and Rubensohn's thick finger traced the last leg of their voyage. His voice was touched with a faint triumph.

"Here is where we are now. Sulawesi to the north. Sumbawa far to the south. Ahead of us—this long island here—is Selajar, which is the gateway to the Banda Sea. Captain Janzoon tells me we shall clear the southern tip about midday today. From there . . ." His finger veered slightly northward and traced a line that bypassed the clutter of islands at the southern tip of Sulawesi and came to rest almost at the center of the Banda Sea. He ringed the area with a pencil and McCreary saw that it was a small archipelago at the center of which lay a largish island. He strained to read the tiny script of the cartographers, but Rubensohn had already given him the name: ". . . We come to our destination—the island of Karang Sharo."

"It's a long way from anywhere," said McCreary.

"An advantage I have not overlooked," said Rubensohn with cool satisfaction. "Technically, the island is Indonesian territory. For all practical purposes, it is controlled by a hereditary sultan, whose power is absolute in Karang Sharo and the surrounding islands."

"And this is where you had your survey made?"

"That's right."

"How did you come to know there was oil there?"

Rubensohn answered without hesitation: "For that I am indebted to Captain Janzoon here. Back in the mid-thirties, the island was listed as a promising survey area by Bataafsche Petroleum Maatshappij. But, with the war, and the later restriction of their franchise by the Indonesian Republic, nothing more was done about it. The record was filed away and forgotten. When Janzoon brought it to my attention, I made overtures to the Sultan, secured his permission for a survey, and later secured a concession, on very favourable terms, from the Government in Djakarta."

"That's the part that interests me," said McCreary mildly. "How did you swing it? I'm an oil man myself, remember, and I know how hard it is even for the big outfits to extend their concessions."

Rubensohn's red mouth twitched into an oblique smile and his eyes sharpened with interest.

"A matter of influence, McCreary. Friends at court, you know."

"Sure," said McCreary softly. "It was a damn-fool question, anyway. By the way, what's the harbour like in this place?"

Rubensohn was watching him now, guarded and suspicious.

"What makes you ask that?"

McCreary shrugged.

"I was thinking of the future: shore installations, storage tanks, harbourage for tankers. It's one thing to pump the stuff out of the ground. You've still got to get it to market. In a place like that—at the rear end of the world—it's a major development project."

Rubensohn frowned and said tersely, "That's not your worry or mine. Our job is to bring in a well."

"Then you sell out as a going concern, eh?"

"Clever fellow," said Rubensohn softly. "Very clever indeed. Looks though we picked the right man, eh, Janzoon?"

Janzoon chuckled asthmatically and slapped a big fist on McCreary's shoulder.

"First time I met him, I told you so, didn't I, Rubensohn? A good fellow, intelligent, far-sighted."

"I like to see where I'm going," said McCreary easily. "Who's the buyer, Rubensohn? Obviously you've got one, otherwise you wouldn't have gone to all this trouble."

Rubensohn wasn't smiling anymore. His mouth was a thin line. His eyes were blank and filmed over like a bird's. His thin bat's voice was edged with anger.

"That's my business, McCreary."

"No!" The word came out, sharp as a whipcrack. "It's mine, too, Rubensohn. I want to know."

Janzoon's mouth dropped open. Lisette's eyes widened with astonishment. Rubensohn and McCreary faced each other, tense and unsmiling, across the table. Finally Rubensohn spoke. He measured out the words carefully, deliberately, like chips on a gambling table.

"You're a driller, McCreary. You are paid to make holes in the ground. The control of any enterprise belongs to the shareholders and directors. If you've any other ideas, I'd like to hear them now."

"Fair enough, Rubensohn." McCreary's brogue was as

creamy as Irish butter. "I'll give 'em to you. You hired me as a driller. I do the job, you lay cash on the barrelhead, no questions asked. That was fine! But you set me up for something else that you didn't tell me about. The way I read it, I need a new contract."

"I don't understand what you mean."

"Do you want it here," asked McCreary gently, "or would you rather have it in private?"

"I want it here and now."

"Good! The man who negotiated your concession in Djakarta was Captain Nasa. I don't know what documents he got you. I don't know how good they are, but I imagine they'll hold water till you get your deal signed up with the buyers and pull out. Nasa tried to hoist the price, so you poisoned him. I walked him off the ship for you and he died in my arms. I left him under a banyan tree about a mile from the dock. Last of all, my name was broadcast over Singapore radio as a probable suspect for his murder. I don't like that. I don't like looking down the barrel like a sitting duck. I think you should tear up my present contract and write me a new one."

Rubensohn's eyes never left McCreary's face. He said in a high whisper, "Get out, Lisette! Get out and stay on deck till I call for you."

She went out swiftly. McCreary held the door for her and closed it again behind her. When he turned back, he saw that Rubensohn held a gun. The barrel was a black, unwinking eye, staring at his heart. Rubensohn was smiling bleakly.

"You're looking down the barrel now, McCreary. Death is very close to you. Have you anything else to say?"

McCreary grinned crookedly. He took out a cigarette, tapped it on his thumbnail and lit it with Nasa's lighter. He blew a cloud of smoke in Rubensohn's face and murmured:

"Put it away, man, and let's get down to business. You

made a mistake. Why not admit it and let's make a new start?"

"And if I don't?"

"Then you'll probably blow the back of my head off. But"—he pointed down at the chart—"you'll have a long, long way to go to find a new driller."

Janzoon mopped his face with his handkerchief and said thickly, "He's right, Rubensohn. Unless we want to upset the whole schedule, we need him. What do we lose if we talk?"

Slowly, ever so slowly, the tension relaxed. Rubensohn laid the gun down on the table and eased himself into a chair. Then Janzoon sat down and, last of all, McCreary. They leaned back, hands on the table edge, eyes downcast, each waiting for the other to make the opening gambit. It was Janzoon who spoke first. His thick voice was unsteady and embarrassed, but he got the words out in the end:

"Maybe McCreary will tell us what he wants. Then we can go from there."

"McCreary?" Rubensohn looked at him with blank, filmy eyes.

McCreary drew placidly on his cigarette for a few moments, then he told them, "The first thing I want is full information on the project, a sighting of all concession documents, a look at all correspondence and cable messages. From here on, you can take it as read that I won't work in the dark. Next, I want a share in whatever company or partnership exists at this moment to control the concession and its working."

"How much?" asked Rubensohn flatly.

"How much is Janzoon getting?"

"Twenty percent."

"I'll take thirty," said McCreary genially. "That still leaves you in control, Rubensohn."

"Anything else?"

"Yes. I'll sit in on all sales negotiations and I'll take my cut from the sale by direct payment from the purchasers."

"And how do you expect to enforce your claims?"

McCreary shrugged and spread his hands in an eloquent gesture.

"Simple enough. If you don't agree, you don't get your oil. If you welsh on me later, I'll tell the buyers a little story about a policeman who was bribed and afterwards murdered. They may not believe it at first, but they'll probably take the precaution of checking with the Ministry in Djakarta. Then they'd find you had nothing to sell." He smiled at them amiably through the smoke. "I gather you'd rather not have that happen?"

Rubensohn's red mouth curled in a grudging smile.

"It's a nice play, McCreary. But you forget one thing. You're outside the law. You're wanted for murder."

"So are you," said McCreary calmly, "though it might take a little longer to prove it."

"It's too much!" Janzoon exploded into guttural anger. "He comes in at the last with nothing more than a threat and he wants more than me—the man who . . ."

"Be quiet, Janzoon!" Rubensohn's peremptory voice cut him short. "McCreary is a good negotiator. He understands that one should always ask something more than one is prepared to accept. Say twenty percent, McCreary, and you're in business."

"Say twenty-five and I'll forget the cruel damage to my reputation."

"No!" Janzoon's cropped head thrust angrily across the table.

"It's a deal," said Rubensohn. "They're my shares, Janzoon, not yours."

Janzoon relapsed into hostile silence.

"Do I get the information and the documents?"

Rubensohn nodded.

"I'll give you a briefcase full of them. You can go through them at your leisure."

"And we'll put all this in writing the way it should be?"

"Before we land on Karang Sharo, yes. Anything else?"

"No, I think that's all."

"Good," said Rubensohn briskly. "Now we can discuss what brought us here in the first place. What happens when we reach the island."

And while Rubensohn went on to discuss the coming operation, McCreary listened with only half his attention. The rest was absorbed by a curious and disturbing question: why had Rubensohn handed a fortune on a silver plate to the man who had it in his power to destroy him?

Even Janzoon didn't seem to know the answer to that one, since for the rest of the meeting he scowled into his beard and said not a single word to McCreary.

Rubensohn, on the other hand, had much to say. His exposition was crisp, concise and businesslike, and McCreary was moved to reluctant admiration for his cool appraisal and his imaginative strategy.

"First, we have our concession from the Indonesian Government. As McCreary astutely points out, this is a dubious document, prized out of a senior official on whom Captain Nasa had an embarrassing dossier. It is, however, quite genuine, although I suspect that the Ministry knows nothing of its existence and the man who issued it will be happy to forget it for a while and repudiate it when it is called in question, by which time we shall have our profit in hand and can leave the legal problems to our successors. Our immediate problem is with the Sultan of Karang Sharo. As I told you, his authority is absolute in his own territory. The folk in Djakarta couldn't control him, even if they wanted to. As it is, they have enough trouble with the rebels in Sulawesi to keep them busy for the next ten years.

"When I first visited the island, the Sultan was well-disposed. He was prepared, for a price, to give us a concession and make labour available for us to work it. Considering the value of the concession, the price is negligible and childish—jewelry, radio sets, assorted European novelties, even a small automobile, though there's hardly a road on the island where he can use it.

"The important thing is that he is a primitive despot. He must be approached with ceremony. We must come as strangers bringing tribute to the man whose title is 'Navel of the Universe.' We'll do that. We'll do it as well as we can. We'll receive him on board and we will be received by him in his palace. Then, after the palaver, we hope to get from him a document under the palace seal, granting us a concession in his own name. Then, if we're lucky, we can start work."

"How long do you expect the junketings to last?"

Rubensohn shrugged dubiously.

"A day, two days, no more. Then you can start unloading the stores and get a permanent camp working. By the way, among the documents I'll give you is a full list of equipment and supplies. You can check it when you have time. I went over it carefully with experts. I think you'll find there's all you want."

"I'm sure I will," said McCreary, and he meant it as a compliment. "So we start work and we hope to bring in a well. When does the buyer come in, and from where?"

"The buyer is Scott Morrison. Do you know him?"

McCreary whistled. Scott Morrison was a big name in the independent oil business. He was a speculator, pure and simple, tabbing the operations of the small concessionaires, ready at the right moment to move in on an outfit that was short on capital but long on promise. He'd buy in on the ground floor, stack up a flotation, hoist the market and move out again, with a three-way profit and no risk except the original gamble. And the odds on that were heavily in his favour. He had the best advice that money could buy and the best nose in the business for a good field.

McCreary chuckled and Rubensohn frowned with irritation.

"Something funny, McCreary?"

"Yes. I just thought of it. Morrison's a filibuster, too, isn't he? He's pulled a few fast ones of his own. I'll be interested to see how you make out."

"How *we* make out," Rubensohn corrected him sharply. "We're partners now, McCreary, remember?"

"I'm not forgetting. I'm just enjoying the joke while there's still a laugh in it. Later it gets serious."

"I'm glad you realize it."

"Where's Morrison now? When does he show up?"

"Cruising," said Rubensohn, with a hint of amusement. "Tahiti, Bougainville, Nouméa, Sydney. Then he's pulling in to New Guinea to take a look at some new operations up the Fly River. We can expect him at Karang Sharo about six weeks from now. If we need him sooner, we can send a radio. He insists on a personal inspection. That's why we must have something to show him."

McCreary grinned.

"He's a wise man. If I were in his shoes, I'd do the same. Do you think he'll take your Djakarta papers at their face value?"

"Give him a smell of oil and he'd take them written on toilet paper. Besides, the mere fact that we're working openly will be proof enough of good faith. All the same"— Rubensohn's full mouth smiled with sardonic satisfaction— "I'd give a lot to see his face when the Indonesian Government orders him off the island."

"You sound as though you don't like him."

"I've done business with him before," said Rubensohn grimly. "Ten years ago, when I was battling for a stake, he turned me out of his office. I've waited a long time to settle the score, but now, I think, we may do it. It depends on you, McCreary."

"I'm glad you said that," murmured McCreary. "It makes me feel better."

Rubensohn looked at him with cool and speculative eyes. He picked up the gun from the table and held it a moment slackly in his hands, then put it back in his pocket. His tone was elaborately casual.

"You play a nice hand, McCreary. I don't grudge you the jackpot. But don't bid too high. It can be dangerous."

McCreary shrugged casually.

"I'm a modest man, Rubensohn. I'm content with a cozy game. So long as it stays that way."

But all the time the black Irish devils were chuckling inside him and he thought, If only you knew, Rubensohn, just how high I am bidding!

# Chapter Six

The next two hours McCreary spent in his cabin, wading through a briefcase full of documents and correspondence which Rubensohn had dumped contemptuously in his lap. The correspondence told him little that he did not know already. Scott Morrison was interested in buying an oil project on Karang Sharo as a going concern after the first proving well had been sunk. Assurances were given that full documentation would be available, and a tentative time had been fixed for a meeting on the well site itself.

What interested McCreary first of all was the fact that none of the correspondence had been signed by Rubensohn. All of it was franked by a certain Joao da Silva, Managing Director of Southern Asia Mineral Research Limited, whose registered address was in Singapore. Rubensohn had been thoughtful enough to include a copy of the memorandum and articles of this company, which showed that it had been incorporated in Singapore twelve months previously and that its directors were John Mortimer Stavey, Wilhelm Kornelis Janzoon and Joao da Silva, each of whom held one share of an authorized capital of £50,000 sterling.

Still no sign of Rubensohn, but that would still mean

nothing. The names were token names, used by the solicitors for the formalities of incorporation. The real information would be contained in the directors' list and the register of shareholders, but of these there was no sign.

The next document was rather more rewarding—as a measure of Rubensohn's confidence, and as evidence of his need for a quick settlement. It was a bill of sale with Southeast Asia Mineral Research as the vendor and Scott Morrison Enterprises Incorporated as the purchaser. It provided for the outright sale of the Karang Sharo oil concession, together with all plans scheduled at the time of signature. Space had been left on all copies for the insertion of monetary figures, and both the document and the space for additions had been signed for the company by Joao da Silva and witnessed by Elisabeth Mary Gonzalez.

There was also a blank space for a second director's signature on the day of completion, and this, he saw with interest, would be Janzoon and not Rubensohn.

The most significant clause in the agreement was the final one: that the sale should become effective on the cabled notification that the purchaser's check had been deposited and cleared to the account of the vendor with the Chase Manhattan Bank in New York.

Once the figures had been agreed, the whole deal could be concluded on the spot and radio messages could be sent off to New York for confirmation and payment.

When that was done, Rubensohn could up anchor and head to sea, richer by several million dollars, leaving Morrison and his lawyers a ten-year battle with the intricacies of international law and the liabilities of corporate bodies registered in foreign territories. Even then, it would be the signatories who would take the rap, not Rubensohn himself. Presumably they considered themselves well paid for the risk. It was fraud on a grand scale, but the odds looked better than even that Rubensohn would get away with it.

The odds were determined, of course, by the final document—the concession granted by the Republic of Indonesia to the Singapore company. This was a fifteen-page opus in Malay, with a certified translation in English, bound in manila and stamped with the massive seal of the Republic—the symbolic Garuda bird, with seventeen feathers in its spreading wings and eight in its splay tail.

There was no doubt of the authenticity of the document itself. The real problem lay in its origins and in the signatures at the foot of it.

Any official with access to files could draw a credible contract, scrawl in the necessary signatures and append the government seal. But if he lacked the authority, the signatures and the seals were of no value to anyone but himself. The man to whom he sold it was risking his whole enterprise on a scrap of worthless paper.

Rubensohn's gamble, however, was based on two very simple pieces of psychology. The first was that he would be working openly and with the personal approval of the local ruler. Even the canniest lawyer would hardly question the legality of his position. The second was that all businessmen mistrust all governments. They resent the restrictions imposed on them by the administrators and they walk in constant fear of the tax collector and the politician. Give them a document signed, sealed and delivered, they are only too happy to lock it in their files and be rid of it.

McCreary smiled with sour admiration at Rubensohn's audacity and astuteness. The man was a filibuster all right—quite amoral, quite fearless. And like so many of his fellows, he stood even chances of ending up with a bullet in his back or with an art collection and a reputation for philanthropy.

Thinking of bullets, McCreary thought of himself and of his all-too-easy victory in Rubensohn's stateroom. He bundled the papers back into the briefcase, lit a cigarette and stretched out on the bunk to consider his own position.

He had cut himself a quarter of the birthday cake, but he had made himself a partner in a criminal enterprise. That was the first bad taste in his mouth. He was a man who had lived rough and loved, at times, unwisely, but so far at least he'd managed to keep his hands clean. Now he was in a dilemma. He wanted to take Rubensohn—take him for his shirt and his girl. But it seemed he couldn't do it without climbing down to the man's own level. There was no immediate answer to this problem, so he pushed it to the back of his mind and hoped that the future might show him some answer to it.

The next problem was less easily shelved. He had to find a way of staying alive.

Until the well was brought in, he was safe, because he was necessary. Afterwards . . . ? He would be not only unnecessary but an active danger to Rubensohn and a pointless charge against the profits. He would be alone, on an island. His only link with the outside world would be Rubensohn's own ship. His only friends . . . then he remembered that he had no friends. He was as rootless as a Galway tinker with no one to care a damn whether he lived or died.

He was still chewing on that sour truth when the door of his cabin opened and Lisette came in.

She closed the door carefully and locked it. Then she came to him swiftly and stood over the bunk. Her face was ashen, her hands were trembling and her voice shook with fear and anger as she blazed at him:

"Why did you do it, McCreary? No matter what happened, no matter what you knew, why couldn't you keep it to yourself? Don't you know he'll never forgive you for what you've just done?"

McCreary took the cigarette out of his mouth and smiled.

"Matter of fact, dark one, I thought he was being

rather pleasant about it. He's given me a quarter share of the business and full director status."

"Dear God in heaven!" Her eyes filled up with tears of impotent anger. "Is there no end to your follies? Don't you know yet what sort of man he is? He may fill your lap with bank notes, your pockets with diamonds, but he'll never forgive you. He'll wait and wait, and one day he'll put a knife in your ribs and twist it till you scream for mercy. But there won't be any mercy. Why didn't you listen to me? Why? Why?"

"Holy Patrick!" McCreary swore softly. "Then you do care! God help me for a bog-trotting clown! You care!"

He heaved himself up on the bed and caught her in his arms and she clung to him desperately, and he felt her body against him shaken with deep, racking sobs.

He held her close to him, his lips brushing her hair, patting and coaxing her like a child in his soft, blarneying voice.

"Come now, sweetheart! Have your cry if it helps, but let's not make an elephant out of a fat toad like Rubensohn. He's not God Almighty, with the power of life and death. There's nothing he can do to either of us, if we've got guts enough to face him."

The words were hardly out of his mouth before she thrust him away again in tearful fury.

"Don't talk like that! I tell you, you don't know him like I do. Look!" She unbuttoned the high-necked Chinese frock and slipped it back from her shoulders.

With a shock of disgust, McCreary saw that her back and her breasts were crisscrosses with thin, angry weals.

"He did that to me last night. He laughed while he did it. He told me it was to teach me that my body was for his pleasure, not for other men to gape at on the deck. Now can you see what sort of man he is? Can you?"

For a long moment McCreary looked at her with pity and tenderness. Then his belly knotted and anger rose in his throat like bile. His eyes hardened and his crooked mouth was as tight as a trap. Very gently he bent and kissed her shoulders, then he drew the frock over them and buttoned it, while all the time she watched him with puzzled, questioning eyes. Then he made her sit down on the bunk while he talked to her, softly, deliberately, in a voice she had never heard before.

"I'm going to take him, Lisette. Not now, not yet, because here, on this ship, I'm as helpless as you are. So I'll smile with him and eat with him and drink with him and let him dream of all the things he's going to do to me after I've served my uses. Then, one day, I'll take him. I'll strip him down, stitch by stitch, till there's nothing left but his yellow soul and his white slug's body. Then I'll kill him for you."

She looked at him with a kind of forlorn tenderness and shook her head.

"You can't, McCreary. Others have tried and they've all ended the same way. He wears his money and his power like an armour. He's too big to touch. He'll kill you before you can get within reach of him."

McCreary gave her a somber, lopsided smile.

"You don't understand the Irish, sweetheart. They're an old dark people, with amazing powers of survival. They saw Herod the Great die with worms in his guts and Nero sobbing for a slave to kill him and the Lord Protector of England pelted to his grave with cabbage stalks and rotten fruit. A man like Rubensohn they can eat for breakfast and still be hungry for bacon and eggs."

He lifted her to her feet and kissed her again, long and passionately, and then sent her to the bathroom to wash the tears off her face so she could greet Rubensohn when he sent for her.

When she came out, her face was the same dead mask that she had shown him the first day they met, but her eyes were warm to him and grateful.

He opened the door to see that the passage was clear,

then he beckoned her out swiftly and watched her go, a small, defiant figure with stripes on her shoulders and the wounds of the world on her heart.

Her perfume still lingered in the cabin and on his clothes, but he paid no heed to it. He lay on the bed with Captain Nasa's lighter in his hands and thought about killing Rubensohn.

Soon after lunch, when all but the duty watch had retired to sleep away the worst of the heat, he climbed to the wireless cabin to talk with Guido. He found the little Neapolitan stripped to his underpants, propped on his bunk, with a glass of beer at his elbow, cigarette in his mouth and a gaudy magazine propped on his knees.

He greeted McCreary with a flashing smile and a theatrical gesture of welcome.

"Come in, *amico*. Get yourself a beer! Sit down and share my women. They're all I have now, but you're welcome to them."

McCreary grinned and swept the magazine out of his hands.

"Save it till you get ashore, Guido! I've known men go crazy with too much reading like that!"

"I don't read!" protested Guido. "I just look and dream and bite my fingers."

McCreary chuckled and eased himself into Guido's chair. He propped his feet on the bunk, lit a cigarette and looked at Guido with quizzical interest.

"Any more news from Singapore, Guido?"

"Nothing." Guido shook his head emphatically. "I take all the transmissions, but nothing more comes in. You think maybe they found the killer by now?"

"I doubt it."

McCreary blew a couple of smoke rings while he considered his next gambit. He needed desperately to trust

71

someone, and the cocky little wireless operator seemed the most likely and the most useful bet. But, if he made a mistake, he was finished. His chances of survival were cut to nothing.

Guido watched him with bright, intelligent eyes. He said shrewdly, "You got something on your mind, *compar'*. You want to talk about it, but you're not sure you can trust Guido. That's the truth, eh?"

"That's the truth, Guido," said McCreary soberly. "If I put myself in the wrong hands, I'm a dead man."

Guido's lips pursed in a soundless whistle.

"That bad, eh?"

"That bad, Guido."

Guido swung his feet off the bunk and sat on the edge of it. He talked swiftly and quietly with eloquent Latin gestures.

"Listen to me, *amico*. I try to explain something. You know what I am—*Napoletano!* You know what people say of us—that we are liars, cheats, that we would sell our own mothers for a packet of cigarettes. It isn't true. If we don't like you—*sicuro!*—we squeeze you for what profit we can make. But if you are *simpatico*, we make you a *compar'*—a pal. We share our bed with you and our pasta and our wine. We hide you from the police or from an angry husband. If there are knives against you, our knives are out, too. You understand that. To me you are *simpatico*. You don't come in here looking down your nose at a cut-off fellow who looks like an Arab. You come with a smile. You drink my beer, I smoke your cigarettes. You call me Guido. So you can trust me, eh?"

"Thanks, Guido," said McCreary warmly.

Then he told him everything from the beginning in Pakanbaru to the last hour in his cabin with Lisette. He told him what he wanted to do and how the odds were

stacked against his doing it. When he had finished, Guido's
face was clouded with anger and his dark eyes were somber.

"*Mamma mia! Che covo di ladri!* What a bunch of
crooks! You are in worse trouble than I thought. Anything
you want, I do, you know that."

"There's nothing you can do yet, Guido. Just keep an
eye on the radio traffic and let me know what goes through.
When we get to Karang Sharo, I'll be working. But I want
you to keep in touch with me—and keep an eye on Lisette.
I'll tell her about you when I get a chance. I only wish I had
a gun."

Guido brightened immediately.

"I got a gun, *amico*. I have not used it since the war,
but I always carry it, in case I meet the wrong girl in the
wrong house, eh?"

He slid off the bunk and fished in a battered suitcase to
come up with a stubby automatic and two clips of ammuni-
tion. The gun was carefully oiled. McCreary tested the
action, shoved a shell into the breech and slipped on the
safety catch. Then he put the gun into his trouser pocket.
His eyes were bright with gratitude as he held out his hand
to Guido.

"Thanks, Guido. I won't forget this. And when we've
taken our profit from Rubensohn's hide, you get your cut,
too."

Guido shrugged.

"Forget the profit. Look after yourself and the girl."
His face brightened into a grin of happy lechery and he
thumped McCreary on the chest. "It shows, *amico!* You can
never guess. A cold one like that and suddenly she is on fire
like brandy on a *bombe!*"

"You've got a dirty mind, Guido," chuckled McCreary.
Then he shoved the little fellow back onto the bunk and
walked out into the raw tropic sunshine. He stood awhile at
the rail, watching the green hump of Selajar receding
westward.

He felt better now. The odds against him had shortened a little. He had allies now—Guido and Lisette—and when he shoved his hand into his pocket, the gun lay hard and comforting against his palm.

# Chapter Seven

The night before they raised the island of Karang Sharo, Rubensohn called a conference of his staff.

McCreary was there, and Lisette, with Captain Janzoon and the ship's officers—all except young Arturo who had the bridge watch. They sat in a circle on the afterdeck under a sky hung with low, soft stars. Rubensohn was in an expansive mood. He brought out champagne and cigarettes and talked with more charm and consideration than McCreary would have believed possible for so gross a man.

Then, when they were at ease with him and with one another, he plunged briskly into business.

"Tomorrow, gentlemen, we make our landfall—Karang Sharo. We expect to spend some time there, six weeks, eight possibly. In the work we shall be doing there, all of you must take a share. All of you will have certain responsibilities in maintaining good relations with the island people, and through them with their ruler. Now . . ." Rubensohn gestured emphatically with his cigar and they bent towards him attentively. "We anchor offshore, because there is no adequate wharf. We have fifty tons of supplies to unload—some of these will be transported in our own lifeboats, the rest will be taken ashore on pontoon rafts which will be ready for us on our arrival."

McCreary looked up sharply. It was the first he had heard of a Rubensohn representative on the island itself. Rubensohn caught his quick, inquiring glance and smiled obliquely.

"A question, Mr. McCreary?"

"No, no! I'm just interested." McCreary waved aside the irony. "I've been asking myself how you were going to get a couple of generators, pumping gear and two thousand feet of casing onto the beach."

"We have someone organizing that for us," said Rubensohn. "His name is Pedro Miranha. He's a half-caste Portuguese from Timor, married to a local girl. He runs a trading post of sorts on Karang Sharo. He speaks the local dialect and some English and stands well with the palace authorities. I've arranged for him to act as interpreter, negotiator and recruiter of local labour. If you, McCreary, or any of you have problems, take them up with him. Is that clear?"

There was a murmur of agreement from the little group.

Rubensohn went on, his high voice tinged with sardonic humour.

"Some of you have visited the island before. You know that the people are mixed migrant stock, from Bali and Lombok, from Sulawesi and from Ceram. The women are beautiful and the men temperamental. You know also that any—er—arrangements for your comfort are best made through Miranha, and that offenses against the family code are liable to have frightening results. For this reason all non-European personnel will be required to report back to the ship before midnight, except those who are detached for duty in McCreary's camp. No women will be allowed on board at any time. We are running a ship, not a brothel. The responsibility for the execution of this order will rest on the officer of the watch. Any breaches of it will be reported immediately to the captain."

"Does the order apply to officers as well?" It was Alfieri who asked the question in his cool, fastidious voice.

"To all officers," said Rubensohn with terse humour. "They can make whatever arrangements they like, so long as they make them ashore and see that they remain fit for duty. Talking of fitness, we have no doctor on board. There is none on the island. Malaria is endemic here, so before we land you will all be issued suppressant tablets, and both the shore party and those living aboard will use mosquito nets at night."

Watching him in the starlight, listening to his crisp, well-reasoned commands, McCreary was touched again with admiration for his genius as an administrator and a strategist. If this was the way he handled all his business, he couldn't fail to make money. If his revenge were planned with equal care, it boded ill for the man he was gunning for. . . . Rubensohn's high voice took up the thread again.

"Our first job is to get the stores ashore and a work camp set up on McCreary's drilling site. Our next is to get the derrick erected and the motor and generators installed and storehouses built. There's enough unskilled labour on the island, but for installation and maintenance, McCreary, you'll be able to call on Agnello and the engine-room staff for whatever help you want."

"The installation's the biggest part," said McCreary. "Once the stuff is running, it's only normal maintenance, barring accidents, of course."

"I hope we won't have any accidents," said Rubensohn coldly.

"So do I," said McCreary blandly. "But they do happen and it's wise to be prepared. We'll be running the motors day and night. I'll want Agnello to have a look at 'em every third day."

The horse-faced Florentine nodded.

"For the beginning, I stay ashore with you. After that I come visiting. How far is this camp from the beach?"

"Three miles," said Rubensohn.

"A damn nuisance without transport," said McCreary. "Every time I want something from the ship, I've got to send a runner."

"Maybe I can help," said Guido.

McCreary looked across at him and caught his flashing smile and the faint suggestion of a wink.

"How?" asked Rubensohn.

"I got two emergency transceiver packs. One of those we can set up on board for me or for the officer of the watch. If McCreary wants anything, he calls up the ship and we organize it. Presto!"

"Suits fine!" said McCreary with enthusiasm.

It suited better than they knew. It gave him a link with Guido, a link with Lisette, who, once he was working, would be too far away from him for comfort. It wasn't so important now, but later his life might depend on it.

Rubensohn nodded agreement and passed briskly to the next part of the agenda.

"Formalities, gentlemen. Our estimated time of arrival is ten-oh-oh hours tomorrow morning. We expect to receive the Sultan and his retinue on board at midday. All officers and crew will be mustered to receive him. Full dress for officers, clean clothing for crew. Captain Janzoon will meet the Sultan and bring him down to the saloon. Then lunch will be served on deck. That's for you, Alfieri—ten, fifteen people in addition to our personnel. Champagne for the visitors, fruit drinks for the rest." He grinned at them sardonically. "This is only the beginning. There is the night to be got through as well. I want no incidents until I've completed certain business with the Navel of the Universe. In the evening, I understand, we'll be received in the palace—officers only, but each man will choose one of the crew to attend him as personal servant. I'd like to make an impressive showing. The ship will be manned by a dock watch of one officer and skeleton crew in engine room and galley and on deck. And that's all, except for a final word from Captain Janzoon."

Janzoon coughed over his cigar and began to talk in his thick voice: "For the lady this is no concern. For the men, all of you, it is very important. I do not make jokes with you, I will tell you the truth. Until the war I lived in these parts most of my life. I know something about these people—and about their women."

He chuckled throatily and went on: "Like Mr. Rubensohn says, we don't mind what sort of entertainment you make for yourselves, so long as you don't make trouble for us. But I give you all a friendly warning. Have yourself a playmate, if you want. But do not take yourself a mistress or a lover. If you do, you find maybe when you come to go home, you can't go. You are lying on the mats in an atap hut retching your guts out because your girl has poisoned your drink or chopped up her hair and put it in your curry. There's no cure for that. You get the biggest bellyache of your life and you bleed inside and you swell up with peritonitis. And don't touch a married woman or you get another sort of bellyache when her husband cuts you up with his kris."

Guido's voice piped up forlornly, "A man should stay with his picture books."

Janzoon smiled grimly.

"He should, my friend, but he won't. So I give you a friendly warning, eh? Sometime, later, I've got to sail this ship. I don't want to sail her short-handed."

There was a ripple of laughter round the deck and Rubensohn signalled to the steward to bring out more champagne. They toasted the enterprise and toasted one another. Then, after a while, Rubensohn and Lisette went below and the rest of them dispersed.

McCreary walked over to the starboard rail and lit a

cigarette. The moon had not yet risen and the ship was a small moving island of light in a dark sea, pricked only by unfamiliar stars and touched, here and there, by faint phosphorescence. There was no land now, no winking signals from passing merchantmen. They were heading northeasterly off the trade routes into the old pirate waters of the Chinese and the Buginese and the Portuguese filibusters. Now they were the filibusters, sailing under the flag of a tatterdemalion republic, on errands far outside the law.

There was a footfall behind him, and a moment later Captain Janzoon's burly figure was propped on the rail at his side.

"A nice night, my friend."

"Sure," said McCreary amiably. "A nice night."

"You should feel very pleased with yourself, McCreary."

"Why so?"

Janzoon spread his big hands in a grasping gesture.

"Why not? The big play—the big profit. You cut yourself in for a lot of money."

"If I don't bring in a well," said McCreary coolly, "there's no money in it for anybody."

Janzoon gave him a quick, sidelong glance.

"Perhaps you'd like to lay off some of the—the risks."

McCreary shrugged with apparent indifference.

"What's the risk for me? Only time and effort. They cost me nothing."

"There's your life," said Janzoon softly. "And the girl's."

McCreary held tightly onto the rail and stared out to sea. The knives were out again, pricking round his ribs. At the first flicker of doubt or fear they would slide in, up to the hilt.

After a long pause he said lightly, "We all take risks, Janzoon—me, Rubensohn, you. It's not so bad if you carry insurance."

Janzoon licked his lips. The conversation was taking an unexpected turn. This lean-faced Celt had more reserves than he had counted on. He tried another maneuver.

"Listen, McCreary! I'm trying to tell you something. There are three of us in this deal: Rubensohn, me and you. Rubensohn's the big one, but you and me together, we are pretty big, too. You see? We should be allies, not enemies."

McCreary slewed round sharply to face him. His voice was low but tight and cold.

"You've given me this before, Janzoon. The big spiel. Friends and neighbours. Brothers in arms! Now let's get some facts on it. I don't like mysteries. I don't like threats. I don't like card games with five aces in the pack. If you've got a proposition, let's hear it—all of it. And let's be blunt! It'd better be good because at this moment you need me much more than I need you!"

Janzoon grinned at him behind the thick spade beard. His eyes twinkled maliciously.

"So! Plain talk you want? The open game? Good! I show you what I hold—three aces!"

"Let's see 'em."

"First, you have a yen for Rubensohn's girl."

McCreary shrugged.

"That's not an ace, Janzoon, that's a deuce. I've had a yen for lots of girls. Not one of 'em was worth a quarter of a million."

Janzoon spread his hands in a wide gesture of disbelief.

"No one asks you to pay so much. You have the want for her. If Rubensohn hears it, he will kill her first and then you. So it comes out an ace anyway, McCreary—the ace of hearts."

"Go on!" McCreary's voice was bleak.

"The next one is the ace of diamonds." Janzoon was enjoying the metaphor. "You asked for thirty percent. You got twenty-five, more than me—and I'm the man who put the thought in Rubensohn's mind. You make what you think

81

is a clever condition. Your share of the money must be paid to you direct. Rubensohn agrees to that, too. You think you have touched the horn of plenty. You bloody fool!" Janzoon's grin changed to a crooked sneer. "You think you know everything. But you know nothing. You don't touch that money till Scott Morrison comes. And Scott Morrison doesn't come till Rubensohn sends for him. He doesn't send for him till the well blows in. Before he comes, you are dead! No pockets in a winding sheet, McCreary. But I can keep you alive—at a price."

"We'll come to the price in a minute," said McCreary easily. "I'm interested in the last ace of yours."

"The ace of spades," said Janzoon. "The gravedigger. You read the documents Rubensohn gave you?"

"I read 'em, yes."

"You read the bill of sale?"

"Yes."

"And the articles of association of the company? You see that Rubensohn's name does not appear in either?"

"I thought that was very clever of him," said McCreary tartly. "He takes the money, but he doesn't take the risk. You're liable for any action that's brought in this part of the world because your name's on the Singapore registration."

Janzoon looked at him in swift surprise.

"So you saw that, too? Good! But did you reason to the next step? Rubensohn's signature is not necessary to the sale. If there are any alterations necessary to the drawn document, I can countersign them under the articles. So maybe it's better if we both stay alive and Rubensohn dies, eh?"

"Holy Patrick!" McCreary swore softly. "That's one I hadn't thought of!"

Janzoon chuckled.

"It makes a nice hand, eh, McCreary? You got any cards to beat it?"

"Depends on which way you want to play it," said McCreary.

"What do you mean?"

"There's three ways, Janzoon. Take your pick. First, I can sit back and bid against you on the strength I hold—and you're still not quite sure what that is. Otherwise you wouldn't be here now. Next, you can buy me out of the game altogether, cash on the nail—here and now. I become a paid employee again, no questions asked; except that I want a very good offer and a guarantee of safety when the job's done, and Lisette would have to be part of the purchase price. Last of all, we play together and against Rubensohn and split the stake fifty-fifty. But understand something . . ." McCreary faced him squarely. His lean jaw was set, his eyes bright with challenge. "I won't be threatened, I can't be scared. I've not got a soul to care whether I live or die, so I can gamble my life with a free conscience. I don't care, you see? I'd like to come out of it with a whole skin and a nice profit, but if I can't, then by the living Harry I'll give you both a hot run for your money! Does that make it plain?"

Janzoon looked at him with sober, speculative eyes.

"Very plain. I think I can make you an offer that will attract you. But I like to think about it first, eh?"

"Does that mean *you'll* think about it or Rubensohn?"

"God in heaven, no!" For the first time, there was real fear in Janzoon's voice. He laid a big hand on McCreary's arm and his fingers bit desperately into the flesh. "At the beginning, sure! I sound you out for Rubensohn. But this, no! This is a private thing. I know how close we sail to the wind. I am not happy about it. I want the profit, but I want the risks better than they are for me. If Rubensohn knew . . ."

"He won't," said McCreary curtly, "so long as you play straight with me. And another thing . . ."

"Yes?"

"Rubensohn lied about Scott Morrison's cruise, didn't he?"

Janzoon looked at him in surprise.

"How did you know that?"

"Easy enough. Rubensohn said he was up the Fly River in New Guinea. That's combine territory, all of it. No interest there for a freelance speculator like Morrison."

Janzoon nodded slowly.

"Rubensohn does that always. He makes a maze of little lies for no good reason. Unless you ferret it out for yourself, he will never give you the real truth. That's one of the things that makes me uneasy now. We are trying to sell a big lie to Scott Morrison and yet Rubensohn still tries to sell little lies to me—his partner."

"Where is Scott Morrison now?"

Janzoon cast a quick, scared glance round the deserted deck.

"He's in Darwin Harbour. He's looking at oil claims in the north of Australia and waiting for word from us."

"How many days' sail from here?"

"Three, four at most. This is the good time in these waters."

"Thanks," said McCreary, in his most genial brogue. "That makes it easier for all of us."

Janzoon seemed suddenly remote and abstracted. He nodded vaguely and stood irresolutely, as if trying to put an uncomfortable thought into words. McCreary lit a cigarette and waited.

After a while Janzoon said uneasily, "I think we can do business, McCreary. I know we should. But—but—there are promises I can't make."

"Such as?"

"The girl. How important is she to you?"

"Why?"

"Because . . ." Janzoon fumbled awkwardly for the phrase. "Because I don't want to spoil our business

. . . because of what Rubensohn may . . . may have in mind for her."

"Do you know what he has in mind?"

"No, but—"

"For God's sake, Janzoon!" McCreary's voice was edgy and impatient. "Out with it, man! What are you trying to tell me?"

Janzoon gestured wearily.

"I try to tell you that if you want her, you fight Rubensohn, not me. If you lose, you blame him, not Janzoon. Do you understand?"

McCreary smiled crookedly.

"Sure! I understand! Women are private business. I'll handle it when the time comes."

"Good!" Janzoon was obviously relieved. "For the rest of it, I think over a figure and terms and I make an offer. Yes?"

"Take your time," said McCreary with a grin. "I'm in no hurry."

But when he was alone again, looking out at the flat sea and the march of the pendant stars, his face grew somber.

Janzoon he could handle, playing on his greed and his fear of Rubensohn. But Lisette was a different matter. He knew now that he was in love with her, and a threat to her was a knife held to his own throat.

# Chapter Eight

"There it is, McCreary! Karang Sharo." Rubensohn's voice was higher than usual with the excitement of the landfall. "Here, take the glasses!"

They were standing on the bridge with Captain Janzoon, watching the island grow from a blur on the horizon to a sharp contour, while Alfieri called to the helmsman the new bearings that would bring them round to the southeastern entrance to the harbour.

McCreary took the glasses and focussed carefully. He saw a long serrated spine of mountains rising slowly to a high truncated cone over which a small mushroom of smoke hung lazily in the still air. He whistled and turned to Rubensohn.

"Volcanic, eh? You didn't tell me that!"

"Is it important?"

"Could be. You might find natural gas instead of oil."

Rubensohn smiled his low, oblique smile and nodded, approvingly.

"You know your job, McCreary. You continue to impress me. It's a question I had already taken up with the surveyors. They tell me the odds are on oil."

"They'd know, of course," said McCreary, with mild irony. "Just thought I'd mention it."

He turned back to scan the approaching coastline. Black cliffs rose sheer from the water, and after the cliffs came mountains coated with smoky greenery, clear to the peaks, except for a small barren area below the mouth of the volcano.

"Nothing on this side," said McCreary. "What's it like on the other?"

"A paradise!" said Rubensohn with enthusiasm. "The mountains break down into foothills and the foothills spread out into a wide, flat plain cut into plantations and paddy fields. There is a gold beach and a circle of harbour fringed with palms and the huts of the fishermen. We have to tack round to come into it through the archipelago."

McCreary raised the glasses again and saw a scattering of smaller islands, jade and emerald, strung out from the southern tip of Karang Sharo. He saw the changing colours where the sunlight lay on shallow reef water and the small shapes of the sails clustered like sea birds over the fishing grounds.

"You see those mountains?" Rubensohn put his hand on McCreary's shoulder and turned him back to Karang Sharo itself.

"I see 'em, yes."

"They are full of swift waters, McCreary—streams that rush down to feed the canals and irrigate the paddy fields. And the streams are full of diamonds. You can pan them like gold. The people will sell them to you for tobacco or betel nut or trade goods. Miranha himself buys a few to sell in Timor, but he is too far away from the market to do very well. You should think about it while you're here."

"I'll do that," said McCreary. "Thanks!"

He handed the glasses back to Rubensohn and stood watching the helmsman bring the nose of the *Corsair* onto the new tack.

Janzoon said tentatively, "Maybe Lisette would like to see this. Something new for her, eh?"

"Women have no taste for scenery," said Rubensohn indifferently, "except as a background for their own beauty."

"I'm going below to have a shave." McCreary's voice was as casual as he could make it. "I'll be back to see us enter the harbour. Like me to knock on the door and tell Lisette where you are?"

"As you wish," said Rubensohn over his shoulder. "And ask her to bring up my sunglasses. I'll need them shortly."

"I'll do that."

He waited a moment longer lest even a suspicion of haste betray him, but Rubensohn was still peering through the glasses at the dragon-like mountains of Karang Sharo. Then he turned away and walked swiftly down the companion ladder.

His heart was pounding when he reached the door of the stateroom. This would be the first private moment he had had with her since she had come to his cabin. They had met, to be sure, at meals and on the deck; but they had been like people shut off from one another by soundproof glass, their conversation soundless, their gestures a meaningless mime. He knocked on the door.

Lisette's voice, glassy and impersonal, answered: "Who's there?"

"It's me—McCreary. Open up, quickly."

There was a moment's pause, then the door opened. "McCreary, what . . . ?"

He moved swiftly inside, closed the door and took her in his arms, stifling her questions with a kiss. Then he released her and talked swiftly and urgently.

"Rubensohn's on the bridge. He wants you up there. Take his sunglasses. I told him I'd look in as I was passing. So I daren't stay more than a moment."

"God, I've missed you!" She came to him again,

fiercely and passionately, drawing his face down to her own, pressing her body against him, then thrusting him away with the same abruptness. "I'm frightened, McCreary. Today is the beginning of it and I'm frightened."

"So am I, dark one," said McCreary. "Frightened for you more than for myself. I've got to talk to you. And this isn't the time or place for it. How can we get together?"

"I've been thinking that, too. Perhaps when we anchor first Miranha will come aboard. They may want to talk privately. If I can get away then . . . ?"

"I'll be in my cabin. I'll wait for you."

"I'll try to come."

"Good. Now get up on the bridge as quickly as you can, and don't forget the sunglasses."

"Kiss me, please."

When the kiss was done, she reached up with her small ivory hands and touched his cheeks and said softly, "It is a small thing, I know, to be loved by a woman from the Peacock Pavilion; but I love you, McCreary. Whatever happens, I love you."

"I love you, dark one," said McCreary gravely. "And nothing is going to happen but good for both of us."

Abruptly as he had come, he left her, and she stood looking at the blank door, wondering how she would bring herself to tell him of the bargain that Rubensohn had proposed to her.

Two steps from the door of Rubensohn's stateroom, McCreary cannoned into Guido, on his way down to the saloon for a late cup of coffee. The dark fellow whistled and wagged a warning finger.

"*Mamma mia!* How crazy can a man be? In full daylight, with the whole ship astir! What happens if it is not Guido but Rubensohn or Janzoon?"

"Shut up, Guido. Come with me. I want to talk to you."

Before he had time to protest, McCreary caught him by the arm and hustled him inside his own cabin.

"I'm thirsty," mourned Guido plaintively. "I got up late. I have a taste in my mouth like old boot leather. I need my coffee."

"You'll get it in a minute," said McCreary unfeelingly. "I want to talk to you."

Guido sighed mightily and sat on the bed while McCreary began laying out his shaving gear and talking to him from the washroom alcove.

"When was the last time you had any radio traffic from Rubensohn?"

"Not since before Djakarta."

"How does he send? In code or clear?"

"In code—it comes cheaper that way."

"What's the code—a private one?"

"No. He uses Bentley's."

"Who does the encoding?"

"Me." Guido reached for one of McCreary's cigarettes and lit it, all unknowing, with a dead man's lighter. "Listen, *compar'!* Maybe we come at this quicker if you tell me what you're driving at, eh?"

"I'm trying to establish two things, Guido. First, if a code message comes in for Rubensohn, can we read it?"

"Sure," said Guido confidently.

"Second, if I want to send a message in Rubensohn's name, can I do it and get away with it?"

"*Senz' altro!* You can get away with it, provided you remember two little things."

"What are they, Guido?" McCreary stuck his head out from the alcove. His face was smothered in lather, but his eyes were bright with interest.

Guido blew a succession of careless smoke rings and gave McCreary a wide, urchin grin.

"All this information and I don't even get a cup of coffee!"

"I'll buy you a bottle of cognac instead. Give, Guido! Give!"

Guido dropped his voice to a stage whisper and told him.

"I pick this up because I am an observant fellow. Nobody tells me. I just see it as the traffic goes through. When he cables Singapore, he begins 'For Silva' and signs himself 'Rex.' When he cables New York, he begins 'For Mortimer' and signs himself 'Imperator.' "

"Rex—Imperator. King—Emperor." McCreary gagged on a mouthful of lather. "That's a little much, isn't it? What does he think he is—Napoleon Bonaparte or God Almighty?"

"From the way he handles his girl," said Guido, "he might be Nerone or Caligula."

"I didn't think you'd know about them," said McCreary, with a wry grin.

Guido made an airy gesture of condescension.

"I got a cabinet of books about them, full of dirty pictures!"

"I wouldn't doubt it for a moment. Now tell me something else, Guido. Have you seen any traffic from Rubensohn to Scott Morrison?"

"Only two messages."

"How were they addressed?"

"Morrison—M. V. *Melanie*."

"And the signature?"

"Asmin."

"Come again, Guido?"

"Asmin—it is a cable address for Southeast Asia Mineral Research, Rubensohn's company."

"No other signature?"

"Oh, yes. Always Janzoon."

"Janzoon?"

Guido nodded emphatically. "I thought it was funny, too, seeing that Rubensohn wrote the messages and delivered them to me. But I am not paid to ask questions. I send them as they come."

"Damn!" McCreary was so absorbed in his questioning that he nicked a neat triangle out of his jaw.

Guido chuckled and said, "Keep your mind on your job, *amico*. I'm still here, and dry as a . . ."

"Get it straight, Guido!" McCreary dabbed his face with styptic and talked rapidly and tersely. "Once we drop the hooks, we're not going to have much time together. From now on, I want a copy of all incoming messages. And hold any outgoing traffic until I've given you a clearance to send it."

"Body of Bacchus!" Guido's eyes popped and the cigarette fell out of his mouth. "You know what you're asking? The incoming stuff—sure! That's easy. But the other? You know what Rubensohn does? He brings it to the radio cabin and stands over me while I code it and send it. I try to help you, McCreary, but this is suicide you want!"

Wiping the last fluffs of lather from his face, McCreary stepped back into the cabin. His lean face split into a lopsided grin and his voice was full of the blarney.

"We can still do it, Guido, and spit in Rubensohn's eye at the same time. Look! You're giving me a transceiver pack for the camp. You're giving me a Morse key, too. We arrange morning and evening schedules to keep in touch. If Rubensohn wants to stand over you while the message goes out—fine! If it looks like normal business, you send the damn thing like a good operator and let me know the contents on the next schedule. But—and this, me bright bandit, is where you must use your judgment—if it looks odd or urgent, or dangerous to me, then you're professional enough to fake a breakdown until you've checked with me. Now, does that make sense or not?"

Guido brightened immediately. His dark eyes sparkled.

"If you talk to the girls like you talk to me, McCreary, you'll never want for a bed. That way we can do it—*sicuro!*"

"Fine!" McCreary reached for the cigarettes and shoved one in Guido's mouth and one in his own. "Now, there's something else. Janzoon has approached me with a proposition."

"What sort of proposition?"

McCreary snapped the lighter and lit their cigarettes before he answered.

"I don't think he's quite clear on it himself yet. But it boils down to two alternatives: buy me out at his own price in return for protection from Rubensohn, or team up with me against Rubensohn and split the profit fifty-fifty."

Guido cocked his head on one side and looked quizzical.

"You know why he makes this proposition, McCreary?"

"I'm not sure, but I think he's scared that Rubensohn is going to sell him down the river."

"I know he is," said Guido simply.

"And how the devil would you be knowing a thing like that?"

"I think it out for myself. You know Alfieri—how he walks about with his nose in the air and his chest stuck out as if he were the Doge of Venice?"

McCreary nodded.

"Last night he was so full of news, he had to share it with someone. He comes to my cabin with half a bottle of grappa and tells me that Rubensohn has sounded him out for the captain's job. Told him Janzoon might be retiring at the end of the trip, going into business. He mustn't say anything, of course. But he has to say it, or burst his breeches."

"Hell and damnation!" McCreary cursed softly. "What's Rubensohn driving at?"

Guido grinned and stabbed a bony finger at his chest.

"Ask me, McCreary! This is the way it goes in Naples. We call it *'schiffo.'* You tell a small truth here and a big lie there. You buy this one a dinner and seduce that one's wife and write a letter to the bishop about the morals of the mayor—and at the end of it everyone is at his neighbour's throat and you walk off with the money and the girl. That's what Rubensohn will do, watch!"

"The hell he will!" said McCreary. "If it's rogues you want and shysters and monumental liars, they come biggest of all inside the ring of Kerry!"

"I'll take your word for it," said Guido dolefully. "Now, please, *amico,* can I have my coffee?"

# Chapter Nine

Now they were threading their way through the outer ring of islands, the slow water curling away from their bow and rocking the small craft that put out from the beaches and the praus that rode with slack sails on the fringe of the reefs.

The beaches were lined with people, bare-breasted women in gaudy sarongs, scrabbling children and small brown men with bright turbans and carved combs in their hair. Behind the people were the roofs of the kampongs peering between the palm boles and the lush green of the undergrowth.

Karang Sharo lay ahead and to port, but the harbour was hidden behind a long flank of hillside that tapered down from the peak of the volcano.

The sky was clear and cloudless and the sun struck back cruelly from the smooth water and made vivid patterns of light and shadow in the folds of the land.

McCreary stood with Rubensohn and Lisette and let the warmth and the colour seep into him. Lisette was cool and remote—her eyes an enigma behind the dark glasses. Rubensohn was elated and voluble. He gestured widely and talked in his high, emphatic voice with an enthusiasm odd and disturbing in so devious a man.

"You see now what I mean, McCreary? The new land of promise? No tax collectors, no policemen, no jacks-in-office sitting behind their papers like shabby kings! There is the sun, the sky, the sea, the land—and all that a man cares to wrench out of it with his own two hands. Where have they all gone, the old adventurers? There are a hundred places like this, waiting like women to be taken, but the adventurers never come. Where are they?"

"It's an interesting question." McCreary's eyes brightened with mischief. "The way I've heard it, some of 'em died of strange diseases, some of 'em died of drink, some of 'em were eaten by cannibals, some of 'em lopped by the public executioner, the best of 'em were killed in the war, and the rest are sitting in Lombard Street with hardened livers and fat cigars."

Rubensohn gave a little high cackle of laughter.

"You're an amusing fellow, McCreary. I should keep you near me always."

"You'd get tired of me," said McCreary blandly. "The Irish make good playmates but uncomfortable bedfellows."

"Do they make good lovers?"

"I'm not a woman," said McCreary softly. "I wouldn't know that."

"What do you think, Lisette?" Rubensohn's voice was barbed with malice.

Lisette shrugged indifferently.

"I know nothing about love."

"A neat point, McCreary!" Rubensohn's red lips smiled, but his eyes were bleak. "Lisette is a woman of some experience. When I met her first, she was . . ."

Janzoon's voice called to them from the helmsman's side.

"We're rounding the cape now. You should see the

harbour in a moment. You'll get a better view from the port side."

As they moved through the wheelhouse to take up their new positions, Lisette brushed against McCreary and he felt the light pressure of her hand against his own. It told him plainer than words:

"He guesses, McCreary. Be careful of him. Don't let him goad you."

She walked ahead of him to join Rubensohn on the port wing of the bridge, but McCreary stayed inside with Janzoon.

Janzoon gave him a swift, warning glance, then began scanning the tip of the cape as it slid toward them.

"Port ten!"

"Port ten!" came the parrot voice of the helmsman.

Slowly they rounded the green finger of land and then, like the dawning of a revelation, the harbour of Karang Sharo came into view.

It was a great semicircle of still water fringed with golden sand. Behind it the land rose slowly, terrace on broad terrace, to the flanks of the hills. The paddy fields were broken by patches of plantation and swaths of jungle and the shining dams and canals of the irrigation systems. The kampongs were spread along the shore fringe and dotted intermittently on the higher ground. The roofs of the huts showed brown and yellow against the flaring green of the vegetation, and the flowers of the flame trees were red flecks on the carpet of leaves.

But most startling of all was the palace. It was built on a broad plateau at the foot of the volcano, and the land before it fell away in a series of hanging gardens bounded by elaborately carved palisades. At the back the volcano cone reared up majestically and the buildings themselves were splayed against it, like the spread tail of a peacock, fretted gold and turquoise and dark amber.

Its windows and terraces stared straight into the

morning sun, but at noon the shadow of the mountain would begin to fall across it, a grateful easement from the equatorial heat.

"Well, McCreary!" Janzoon looked at him and chuckled huskily. "What do you say to that?"

McCreary shook his head.

"What do you say? It's beautiful—and the man who designed it was a genius."

"Join us, McCreary!" Rubensohn's high voice summoned him into the sunlight. "I told you I would show you wonders. Now do you believe me?"

"I never doubted you," said McCreary dryly. "It's a great and marvellous thing, to be sure. Like a goldsmith's work."

"And there are as many wonders inside," said Rubensohn with relish. "There are rooms for a hundred concubines and their children. There are state chambers and a hall for the dancers and a theater for wayang puppets. There are painters and musicians and masters, for the girl dancers and the royal treasures are housed in tunnels driven right into the mountain itself."

Rubensohn's eyes glittered behind the dark sunglasses. It was as if he were describing the fulfillment of his own dreams, the proper climax to the career of every filibuster.

More from resentment than from immediate interest, McCreary changed the subject. He said, "Where will I be drilling?"

"Over there!" Rubensohn pointed northward, away from the palace to where a secondary range of hills broke into the terraces and formed a small re-entrant with the main range. "There's a road that runs along the bay to the mouth of the valley. That's the way your stores and equipment will go in. It's away from the main villages, as you see. You'll have a certain amount of privacy."

"Looks as though we'll need it." McCreary pointed to the beach, which was crawling like an anthill with a colourful press of people. Canoes were being pushed off the beach and brown bodies were clambering into them, while small boys and girls plunged into the water and began swimming out to the ship. A figure in white ducks was standing on the spindly jetty and waving frantically. Rubensohn waved back.

"That's Miranha. He'll be out as soon as we're anchored."

As he spoke, they heard Janzoon ring down to cut the engines, and then they were sliding, with way on, through the flat water, while the men in the bows waited for the signal to let go the anchor.

Janzoon bellowed an order and the hooks went down, and the engines started again to make head and take up the slack of the chains. The bell rang again—"Finished with engines"—and they were riding at anchor in the slack water with that curious feeling, half suprise, half disappointment, that comes with the last landfall.

McCreary and Lisette looked at one another. Rubensohn stood a long moment, staring up towards the palace and the smoking mountain. When he turned back to them, he was smiling and rubbing his thick hands together. He chuckled shrilly.

"The overture is finished. Now the opera begins. I hope you both enjoy it very much."

"I'm sure we will," said McCreary. "I know the producer. He's very competent. And besides, he's got a very good leading lady."

Rubensohn flushed with sudden irritation and snapped at him.

"You're impertinent, McCreary!"

"I am, I know that," said McCreary cheerfully. "But I'm also a damn good driller, and a man who's good at his job can afford to speak his mind."

Rubensohn opened his mouth to speak, then closed it again. A wintry anger seemed to take possession of him.

His eyes filmed over and the big beaked nose clamped down over his small feminine mouth. Deliberately, he turned his back on McCreary, linked his arm in Lisette's and stood watching the small white figure of Miranha stepping off the jetty into a shabby motor launch manned by a pair of Sharo boys in batik sarongs.

McCreary propped himself against the bulkhead and lit a cigarette. Then he, too, turned away and strolled into the chart room, where Janzoon was talking to Alfieri. They were stripping the chart from the navigator's table and locking the instruments away. Their work was done, it seemed. His own was just beginning.

The launch ground awkwardly against the plates of the *Corsair*, and a moment later Pedro Miranha came scrambling up the monkey ladder. Rubensohn and Janzoon received him on the bridge, while Alfieri stood at Lisette's elbow and McCreary waited in the background and studied the newcomer.

He was a skinny, narrow-faced fellow with a turned eye and a malarious complexion. His teeth were stained with betel and his thinning hair was plastered across his scalp with palm oil. His hands were knotted and stained and the threadbare ducks hung on him like sacking. His English was surprisingly good, but his voice was a rasping whine and, as he talked, he shifted nervously from one foot to the other.

"Good morning, gentlemen! Welcome to Karang Sharo. A big day for the island. Everybody is out, as you see. Even from the palace they will be watching. Everything's ready for you. . . ."

"Did you get the pontoons built?" Rubensohn asked curtly.

"All built, ready to haul out. Four of them—solid logs underneath and a bamboo decking. Fifteen feet square, take anything!"

"Good! You've got labour lined up for us?"

"Labour!" Miranha giggled foolishly and flung out his skinny arm. "Look at it! Men, women and children. You've only got to whistle and they'll come like ants."

"When can we start unloading?"

"Oh, for that"—Miranha wagged a cautionary finger—"best wait till you've paid respects at the palace."

"Is anything wrong?"

"No! No! No! Nothing wrong, only . . ." He dropped his voice to a confidential whisper. "But you know the way it is up there. We're the Navel of the Universe. We like to be tickled to make us feel better. You've brought the . . ."

Rubensohn cut him short with a gesture.

"Yes, I've brought everything. We can talk about it below. Janzoon?"

"Yes?"

"You and Miranha come down to my cabin. There's a lot to talk about."

Without a word to Lisette or McCreary, he turned on his heel and walked down the companion ladder. Miranha and Janzoon followed him, leaving McCreary and Lisette with Alfieri.

McCreary said quietly, "Now, there's a dock rat, if ever I saw one!"

Alfieri stiffened and said coldly, "Miranha is an important person on the island. Mr. Rubensohn has great confidence in him. He has connections at the palace and . . ."

"They always have," said McCreary contemptuously, "at the tradesmen's entrance and the back door to the women's quarters. He's got a pimp's face and a huckster's eyes. I don't like him."

"You,, of course, have much more experience of such people than I."

It was a patent insult, but McCreary took it with a grin. He said in his gentlest brogue:

"You should relax more, Alfieri. I've known men grow ulcers worrying the way you do. You're not captain yet, and if you're not nice to your friends you never will be!"

Alfieri flushed angrily and stammered.

"I—I don't understand what you mean."

"I think you do," said McCreary softly. "Mr. Rubensohn has been dangling promotion in front of your nose, like a carrot to a donkey. But Lisette here will tell you, there's a long way to walk before you reach it. That's right, isn't it, Lisette?"

Lisette laid a restraining hand on his arm.

"Please, McCreary, let us have no unpleasantness."

"I'm not being unpleasant, dark one. But Alfieri is young and innocent. I've seen fellows like him taken for their shirts because they gambled in the wrong company. Take a tip from me, Mister Mate. Don't believe everything the owners tell you. And don't count on promotion till you've got the braid on your arm and your backside in the captain's armchair."

Then, while Alfieri was still goggling at him, he linked his arm in Lisette's and led her down the companion ladder and towards his own cabin.

With the door closed and bolted behind them, they clung together for a long moment, and McCreary was amazed at the pent passion in her small doll-like body. Slowly they relaxed and McCreary made her sit down on the bed beside him.

He took her hands in his own and said gravely, "There's a lot to talk about, dark one. Let's get that over first."

"I know that, Mike." It was the first time she had used his Christian name. "But first I want you to listen to me."

"Sure, I'll listen. I like your voice better than my own. What do you want to tell me?"

"Give me a cigarette, please."

He opened a new pack, handed her a cigarette and lit

it. She smoked greedily for a few moments, then she began.

"He guesses about us, Mike."

McCreary nodded.

"I gathered that, on the bridge. Has he said anything to you?"

"Not in so many words. But you know how he is—secretive, probing, waiting for the moment when he can hurt most."

"I know, yes."

"He wants to destroy you, Mike."

"I know that, too," said McCreary simply. "But he can't do anything until I've brought in a well for him. And before that I hope to make a few arrangements of my own. That's what I want to talk to you about. I'm going to . . ."

"Please, Mike! Let me talk first."

There was so much urgency in her voice, so much pain in her eyes, that he had no choice but to let her go on.

"I want to tell you about myself, Mike. I want so much that you should understand. If you don't understand, you will do something foolish, something that will be no profit to either of us."

"Before you go on, Lisette . . ." McCreary's voice was grim. "I'll tell you bluntly. What touches you touches me. If I have to blast our way out of this rat hole, I'm going to do it and take you with me."

"I know, Mike, I know. But please . . . please listen!"

"Go ahead, sweetheart."

"I told you where Rubensohn found me—in the Peacock Pavilion in Saigon. I never told you how I came there."

"I've never asked to know."

"But I want to tell you. I did not belong to Saigon. I was from the north—Haiphong. My husband was an official of the French administration."

"Your husband?" The word shocked him like water splashed in his face.

Lisette nodded simply.

"His name was Raoul Morand. He was a *métis* like myself, half-French, half-Tonkinese, so that when the war started and Ho Chi Minh's army moved down from the north, we were not evacuated. We joined the refugees moving south. We made it, too. We came to Binh Dinh and even found a modest lodging outside the town. Raoul went out each day to try to make contact with a French official with power to give him back his old job. Then, one evening, the soldiers came—three of them, from the Binh Xuyen. They were looking for spies, they said. And they stood Raoul against the wall and made him watch while they stripped me. They mocked him all the while and told him what they were going to do to me and, when he tried to break away and help me, they shot him. Then, when they had finished, they took me with them to Saigon and sold me to the Peacock Pavilion, because the Binh Xuyen collected the revenues from such houses for Bao Dai, and his troops stocked them and controlled them for him. I was alive, though I did not wish to be. But after a while I began to be grateful even for that small mercy. Then, one night, Rubensohn came and was pleased with me and offered to take me away. He bought me from the Pavilion for a big price and made me his mistress, and I have travelled with him ever since."

"Is that all, dark one?" McCreary's voice was somber.

"No, it is not all!" Her eyes were bright with challenge. "There is a moral to my story, Mike, I want to read it to you. First I will tell you, truthfully, that even in the Peacock Pavilion one can be grateful for the gift of life. And then I will say that when Raoul died for me, he did a useless thing. Had he not tried to help me, had he been able to bear what they were doing to me, we might have been together now. I might never have come to the Peacock Pavilion, and there would have been nothing but the memory of that one night, and, in time, we might have forgotten even that." Her voice rose sharply and she reached out and grasped his hands again, desperately. "Death is so pointless, Mike! It is the end of hope, the end of love for the one who is left. So that's what I want you to promise me . . . whatever happens, whatever Rubensohn tries to do to hurt me, you will stay alive. Will you promise, Mike?"

"I promise, sweetheart," said McCreary softly.

His arms went round her and drew her to him so that her head was pillowed on his breast, her small, perfect body pressed against his own. But for all the love he poured out on her, she could not bring herself to tell him the truth.

# Chapter Ten

Just before noon Miranha went ashore again, and shortly afterwards the Navel of the Universe came to pay his state visit to the *Corsair.*

They saw him first a long way off, carried in a golden palanquin on the shoulders of ten men along the terraces of the palace, then down the winding path to the flatlands. There were guards in front of him and behind, each with a kris strapped between his shoulder blades and a long musket of ancient design over his shoulder.

The procession lost itself in the green overhang and they did not see it again until the crowds on the beach parted suddenly, fell to their knees and uttered a long, wailing cry that drifted faintly across the water. From the mouth of a canal a long canoe with a carved prow shot out, propelled by ten oarsmen. When they came to the opening in the crowd, they beached it swiftly and the Navel of the Universe was carried down to it on the shoulders of his servants. When he was seated, the courtiers joined him, one of them holding a large yellow umbrella over his head.

Then the canoe shoved off and the oarsmen drove it swiftly with long sweeps of the big, carved paddles.

The gangway was down and a Malay seaman stood with

a boathook to bring the visitors neatly alongside. Arturo waited on the lowest step to hand the visitors aboard. The rest of the ship's company lined the deck, the officers in freshly starched uniforms, the seamen and the lascars and the galley staff all dressed in their shore clothes and standing stiffly at attention. Janzoon and Alfieri were posted at the top of the gangway, but neither Rubensohn nor Lisette were to be seen.

McCreary thought it was another piece of shrewd stage management. The Navel of the Universe must be brought to the great man, alone, in the privacy of the saloon. Lisette would be displayed as a prize possession. It gave him grim satisfaction to think that soon this fiction, too, would be destroyed and Rubensohn would lose Lisette with all the rest.

When the small procession reached the top of the gangway, McCreary saw, with a shock of surprise, that the Sultan was a young man—thirty at most—with finely chiselled Balinese features, set now into a rigid ceremonial mask. He was as colourful as a jungle bird in his ceremonial silks, embroidered with threads of silver and gold. There were jewels at his throat and on his fingers. A dagger with a golden haft was thrust into his sash, and in the center of his round skullcap a great ruby glowed with dull fire.

Behind him came a fat figure, who looked more like a Chinese than a Malay and whom McCreary took to be the vizier. His silks floated about him like a widow's drapes, but his slant eyes were shrewd and appraising. The rest of the courtiers were small brown men, like their master, and their costumes and their jewelry were in descending order of magnificence.

When they reached the deck, Alfieri called the officers to attention and the crew bowed deeply. Captain Janzoon saluted formally, then held out his hand and made a short speech in Malay.

The Sultan made a curt acknowledgment and Janzoon

led the party down to the saloon. Alfieri hustled the crew about their business of setting the afterdeck for the meal, and McCreary and Guido strolled forward to smoke a private cigarette.

Guido quizzed him shrewdly.

"You're a shareholder now, McCreary. Shouldn't you be down there when the business is being done?"

McCreary shrugged off the question.

"The business was done a long time ago, Guido. This is ceremony. Each telling the other what a big shot he is and waiting to see the size of the glory box."

"But the girl is there—your girl."

"She's not all mine—yet. We both know we've got to wait and plan for that, Guido."

Guido gave him an odd, sidelong look.

"You said that like a man in love."

McCreary turned on him sharply.

"What the hell do you think I am?"

"I don't know." Guido made a wry mouth and looked at McCreary with puzzled eyes. "I know you have a want for her; sure, I know you get some satisfaction when you take her from a *maledetto* like Rubensohn. But love! That's a serious thing, *amico*. Love reaches higher than the belly and stabs like a sharp knife. I'm sorry for you."

"Why sorry?"

Guido shook his head.

"The world is full of women—and you fall in love with a packet of trouble. Tell me"—he changed the subject abruptly—"has Janzoon made his proposition yet?"

"No. Not yet. He's waiting to watch the cat jump. So far there hasn't been a real trial of strength between me and Rubensohn. Janzoon will wait for that."

"I don't think he will have to wait long."

There was a note in Guido's voice that brought McCreary up short. The little Neapolitan wasn't joking anymore. His face was puckered with doubt and indecision. McCreary questioned him bluntly.

"There's something on your mind, Guido. Let's have it!"

"No!" Guido was quite definite in his refusal. "I have a thought, but it is mine and private. If I am right, you can do nothing about it. If I am wrong, then you fret for nothing when you should be attending to other things. But this I tell you. If I am right, the first trial of strength with Rubensohn will come tonight."

And with that McCreary had to be content. Before he had time to ask another question, there was a babble of voices on the deck and Captain Janzoon appeared with the vizier and the courtiers of Karang Sharo. The Sultan was still below with Rubensohn and Lisette.

For the next two hours they stood, sat or lounged under the awning, entertaining the visitors, while the galley staff bustled round with dishes and trays of drinks. The officers spoke only shipboard Malay and the brunt of the conversation fell on Janzoon and McCreary, but their patience soon frayed under the grinning politeness of the envoys, who gave oblique answers to their simplest questions and made not a single contribution of their own.

When, halfway through the affair, Rubensohn and the Sultan appeared, the situation was even worse. The attendants stood in attitudes of submission while the Navel of the Universe ate and drank and talked only to Janzoon and Rubensohn.

McCreary stood it as long as he could, then tried to slip away to see what had happened to Lisette. But Rubensohn caught sight of him and called him back to present him to the Sultan, and from then till the end of the ceremony he was anchored, sweating and uncomfortable, trying to answer a hundred questions on the mechanics of oil search, with a vocabulary limited to bed, board and the simpler transactions of living.

Then, finally, it was over. They were mustered again for leave-taking and the royal party was shepherded down into the big canoe. But before they were halfway to the shore, hatch covers were off and Alfieri was standing by the winches to superintend the unloading of the gifts that were to be presented at the evening's reception in the palace.

They heard the put-put of Miranha's launch and saw him towing a string of rough pontoons, each loaded with a bunch of boys to unhook the slings and settle the freight for its journey back to the shore.

Rubensohn kept Janzoon and McCreary with him until he was satisfied with the way the work was being handled. Then he said briskly:

"We have business to talk, gentlemen. Let's go to your cabin, Janzoon. Lisette is resting, I don't want to disturb her. She will want to look her best for the evening."

McCreary looked at him quickly, but there was no malice in his eyes. Rubensohn was at his best when there was work to be done. The mischief and the malice were playtime indulgences. They could not be allowed to interfere with the project in hand.

Janzoon settled them in the cabin and poured three tots of whisky from his private store. He and Rubensohn lit cigars and McCreary smoked a cigarette. Rubensohn came quickly to the point.

"We're a going concern, gentlemen. The Sultan is happy with the gifts we've offered him and with our promise of a royalty on the oil produced, to be paid in kind and in American bank deposits."

"Which he'll never get, of course," said McCreary dryly.

"Precisely!" Rubensohn waved his cigar. "But by the time he finds that out, we'll be away with a profit in hand. Then Scott Morrison can start worrying."

Janzoon chuckled asthmatically.

"I like that touch. The final nail in the coffin, eh?"

Rubensohn hurried on.

"The document of concession will be presented to us tonight at the palace. It has no value in law, but in fact it will be one more piece of evidence to present to our friend Morrison. And he can raise no question of its authenticity."

"When can I start unloading my stores?" asked McCreary.

"First thing in the morning. Miranha will be out at sunrise with his barges. He'll take the crated stuff first. The rest he will leave until you're on deck to superintend, which I imagine will be much, much later."

"What makes you say that?"

Rubensohn sipped his whisky and smiled at him over the rim of his glass.

"Because tonight, McCreary, you will see yet another of the wonders I promised you. We are to be entertained in the palace. We shall be carried up the hill in litters, feasted, entertained and presented each with a royal gift, and carried back again, I suspect, somewhat the worse for wear."

Janzoon spluttered happily over his cigar.

"Watch out for the palm toddy, McCreary. However they spice it, whatever they serve it in, it carries a hundred headaches."

"I'll remember," said McCreary with a grin. "It sounds like the biggest come-all-ye of the season."

"Bigger than you dream, McCreary."

Rubensohn turned to Janzoon.

"A change in orders, Captain. At least until other arrangements can be made onshore, officers will be permitted to bring women aboard ship."

"Is that wise?" Janzoon frowned and looked puzzled. "I like my fun as much as any man, but I like a clean ship better."

"Unless you've any other suggestions? I am informed by the Sultan that each officer will be presented with a concubine for his use during our stay in Karang Sharo." He smiled and licked his red lips. "An ancient custom, I believe, which has, unfortunately, fallen into disuse in other parts of the world. I thought it unwise to refuse, but I must depend on you, Janzoon, to see that discipline is maintained and that suitable arrangements for shore residence are made as soon as possible. We're doing well, McCreary, don't you think?"

"Too damn well," said McCreary without enthusiasm. "Why take so much trouble with a bunch of interlopers who are getting a damn good bargain anyway?"

Rubensohn brushed the objection aside with an airy gesture.

"Perhaps I'm a good negotiator. Perhaps the Navel of the Universe has made a better bargain than he expected. In any case, who are we to complain?"

"Who indeed?" said McCreary dubiously. But, remembering Guido's warning and Lisette's desperate plea, he was troubled and afraid. The prospect of the evening's celebration gave him no pleasure and he wanted desperately to talk to Lisette. But Rubensohn and Janzoon kept him talking through the afternoon. When the time came to dress, Lisette was still in her cabin and Rubensohn was with her, so they had no chance at all to see each other.

The sun went down swiftly behind the spine of the mountains, and at a single stride darkness came down on the islands and on the sea. The stars pricked out, and the yellow lanterns in the kampongs, and the glow of the volcano was spread softly against the night sky.

Then, as if at a signal, the torches were lit—on the beach first, then all the way up the winding path and along the climbing terraces of the palace. Their flames tossed and waved in the hands of the torchbearers, so that it seemed as if a long, fiery serpent were writhing down the mountainside.

When McCreary came on deck, dressed for the evening, he found the other officers on the deck watching the display, stiff as pouter pigeons in mess jackets and starched whites and scarlet cummerbunds.

The gangway was down and the boat was bobbing below it, with the oars shipped and the bos'n standing below, waiting to hand them aboard. Each officer had a crew member allotted to him, and these stood apart, self-conscious in their clean clothes, their eyes rolling with excitement, their voices a sibilant whisper in the shadows.

Alfieri stepped up to him and said curtly, "Captain's compliments, Mr. McCreary. You will go ashore in the first boat with the other officers. Litters will be waiting for you and you will proceed immediately to the palace. Your servant will walk beside the litter and will stand behind you during the ceremony."

He called a name, and a moonfaced Chinese cook boy stepped forward to attend McCreary.

Guido sidled up to him and said softly, "I'm in the first boat, too, McCreary. I'd like to stay near you."

"Suits me fine, Guido. I'm in need of company."

"I thought you might be."

Then Alfieri summoned them crisply and they filed down the gangway, with their attendants following, into the waiting boat.

When they came to the beach, they found the litters drawn up between the lines of torchbearers, and behind the lights they could see the gifts piled for the pack carriers and covered with cloths. Under one of the covers McCreary made out the shape of a small car lashed to long, stout poles for its passage up the mountain. Farther away stood a line of palace guards holding back a press of people whose murmur was like the buzzing of a hive of bees. The torchlight flickered on their shining brown faces and made queer highlights on their goggling eyes.

A litter bearer touched McCreary lightly on the arm

and pointed to his place. McCreary climbed awkwardly onto the platform and seated himself on a low chair covered with patterned silk that smelt of spices and sandalwood. Ahead of him he saw Guido being hoisted awkwardly into his place.

Then, at a word of command, the bearers bent and lifted the long poles onto their shoulders, and McCreary found himself riding high above the torches like a captain in some barbaric triumph.

All the way up the mountain there were the lights and the people. The lights were scented with incense and the incense mingled with the smell of the people and the dust and the warm exhalation of the kampongs and the jungle.

Above him the trees hung slack in the heavy air, and over the leaves were the sky and the soft, low stars. Sometimes he heard the clatter of night birds, but it was a small sound against the cries of the villagers, who laughed and shouted and beat their hands as the guests of the Sultan passed by.

Once the torchlight fell on a broad stretch of water banked on the hillside, where great lily pads gleamed and the giant flowers were folded for sleep, and, because the people were rarer now, he heard the deep drone of insects coming to the lights and the croak of frogs in the green water fringe.

Ahead of him, Guido turned and clasped his hands above his head and shouted back, *"Che passeggiata, amico!* You enjoying yourself?"

McCreary waved and called a warning.

"Watch yourself, Guido! You'll fall off and break your damned neck."

Then, abruptly, they were at the gates.

Two great pillars of teak reared themselves up, sculptured with flowers and writhing monsters and capped with the spread wings of birds. There were guards at each pillar and they waved the procession forward, and as they passed,

McCreary saw the big wooden gates, carved as intricately as a pair of screens, and beyond them the climbing gardens, tier on tier, through which they must pass to the palace itself.

There were lights at every window and in every arch and colonnade so that the fretwork of stone seemed featherlight, apt to blow away in the first wind. But there was no wind. The air was heavy with flowers and burnt incense and a faint, tinkling music of gamelan bells.

Lulled by the swaying of the litter, McCreary felt that he was floating disembodied in an opium dream, incapable of decision or action.

Then, at last, the dream ended.

The procession stopped. The litters were lowered to the ground and, as they stepped out stiffly, they found themselves in a wide, open courtyard, at the end of which a flight of steps led up to the glowing fretwork of the palace. At the top of the steps stood the fat vizier, waiting with a retinue to greet them.

Slowly they mounted the steps, their servants walking a step below them. The vizier greeted them in soft Malay and led them through the portico, along an elaborate colonnade carved in Hindu fashion and into a huge chamber lined with pillars, at the end of which was a raised throne backed by a fretted stonework screen.

They looked at each other, dumb with amazement.

The hall was large enough to deploy an army. The walls and the pillars and the throne itself must have been carved by the craftsmen who came in the ninth century with the Hindu rulers of the Spice Islands.

The center square was brightly lit and set round the edge with piled cushions and low tables of carved wood and pearl inlay. In the shadows behind the pillars, servants in embroidered blouses and colourful sarongs waited silently and, to the left of the throne, a gamelan orchestra played its tinkling monotonous rhythms. From behind the stonework screen came a murmur of women's voices and an occasional smothered giggle, as if the women of the household were watching the arrival of the strangers.

The floor in front of the throne and between the tables was clear to allow the passage of the servants and the entertainers, and the throne itself shone with changing lights as the jewels reflected the wavering flames of the lamps that hung from the ceiling and from the pendants on the pillars.

On the right of the main throne a smaller one had been raised, less richly jewelled, obviously movable. McCreary wondered whether it had been set for Rubensohn or for the senior member of the household. There was no firm protocol in these petty sultanates. Their customs were a baroque compound of migrant manners and strangely mixed faiths.

The vizier led them to the row of cushions immediately facing the throne and seated them a little to one side of the center trio. Guido squatted next to McCreary and watched wide-eyed as the vizier clapped his hands to bring a small troupe of servants, each carrying a tray of beaten silver on which was palm liquor in a silver goblet and a box of strange sticky sweetmeats.

They bowed, presented their offerings and withdrew. As they sipped the sweet, flat liquor, Guido chuckled impishly.

"Poor Arturo! Left with the dogwatch on a night like this. I weep for the boy."

"He's better out of it," said McCreary with a grin. "I'm told it can turn into a willing evening. Where's Rubensohn, I wonder?"

Guido shrugged theatrically.

"He'll be here! The big entrance, with Janzoon in all his gold braid and your girl on his arm. I wouldn't be surprised if he marched straight to the throne and took over from the Sultan."

"I wouldn't either," said McCreary. "But not tonight."

Guido grinned and turned away, chattering in Italian to the other officers. McCreary sipped his liquor and surrendered himself to contemplation of the barbaric splendour around him.

Now, he thought, he could understand the dreams of the filibusters. This was the thing that had beckoned them out, century after century, under alien flags, in leaky ships, with tatterdemalion crews—this vision of peacock thrones and gods with jewels for eyes, and treasure stores under the foundations of fairy palaces.

For them, power was a tangible thing, measured by weight of bullion, by number of slaves, by the size and splendour of palace or mausoleum.

They were the primitives, stifled by civilization. There was no rest for them in the cities, no hope for them in the old world. And if they died too soon, they died with incense in their nostrils and the music of strange tongues in their ears.

Rubensohn had that streak in him and it was the best part of his complex character. It showed in his moments of exaltation and in the cool daring of his roguery. He was a big man; he might even have been a great one but for the taint of cruelty and perverted cunning.

The music stopped suddenly, then began again on a new and stronger beat. There was a rustle of draperies and a murmur of voices and the courtiers filed in, gaudy as parrots in silk blouses and embroidered vests and sarongs stencilled in bold jungle designs. They bowed formally and showed their betel-stained teeth in a grin of welcome, then took their places on the cushions at either side of the hollow square. The servants came forward again with the drinks and the sweetmeats, then withdrew into the dim arches.

A moment later the vizier entered again. Rubensohn, Janzoon and Lisette followed him.

The beauty of her was breathtaking. Her small body

was clothed in a sari of gold, draped ceremonial fashion over her hair and falling in soft folds to the golden sandals. There were emeralds at her throat and on her wrists, and her skin glowed like alabaster with the light behind it.

Her face was a sculptor's mask, immobile, perfect, in which her dark eyes were the only sign of life.

Rubensohn and Janzoon led her to the center cushion and settled her comfortably. Then she drew her sari round her face like a veil and sat, silent and absorbed, waiting for the ceremony to begin.

The fat vizier moved to the foot of the throne and stood waiting. Then a gong sounded, brazen and terrible, echoing through the colonnades and up among the sculptured figures on the ceiling. The whole assembly stood up and waited with bowed heads and closed eyes, while the vizier chanted the ten ceremonial names of the Sultan of Karang Sharo, ending with the greatest name of all—Navel of the Universe.

When they looked up, he was standing on the dais, a small boyish figure against the spread of the peacock throne, with his guards ranged about him and the chair at his side still vacant. He sat down. The company waited till he had raised his hand, and they, too, settled themselves on the cushions.

McCreary thought it was a pretty piece of stage management. He wondered whether Rubensohn had had a hand in it. He also wondered when they were going to bring more drinks. His mouth was dry and the cloying taste of the sweetmeats was still on his tongue.

Then the fat fellow took the floor again.

He spoke, he said, unworthily in the name of the great, whose voice was a thunder that might wake the sleeping mountain. His voice—which he prayed might be like flowers in his mouth—was raised to welcome the strangers whose coming would bring prosperity to the land and wealth to the people. They came as friends, bearing gifts, which were the promise of greater gifts. But the great one, he of the ten names and the greatest name of all, was not to be outdone in generosity. So now to each of the strangers he would give his own gift, a jewel to wear on his heart, a flower to perfume his pillow. . . .

He raised a pudgy hand and the gongs sounded again, and from the shadowy colonnade came seven girls, small and perfect, bright as blossoms, bearing each a small cushion on which lay a jewel set in the soft filigree of the local craftsmen. They came and knelt in front of Rubensohn and McCreary and each of the officers and tendered the gifts. Then they knelt beside the cushions in attitudes of submission to their new masters.

The gongs sounded again and Rubensohn stood up. McCreary watched him, fascinated. Hate him as you might, there was no denying the power that went out from him. His clothes were drab beside the bright finery of the Asiatics, yet he dominated the assembly and seemed even to dwarf the figure on the peacock throne. He paused a moment and then began to speak in perfect Malay, full of allusion and hieratic hyperbole.

He was grateful, he said, for the princely honours done to him and to his friends. The gifts he had brought were small and unworthy beside those of the Sultan, but they were a promise of greater ones. Moreover, they came from a new world, where wonders sprang up like mango trees from the hands of a magician . . .

As he spoke, the servants began carrying the gifts from the rear of the hall and ranging them a little to the side of the throne.

There was a box which would bring the voices of the world into the palace of Karang Sharo. There was a machine which would light the whole palace at the touch of a finger. There was a palanquin on wheels which would carry the Navel of the Universe wherever he wished, as soon as roads were built to accommodate it. There were guns for the royal armoury and glassware such as the princes of Europe used. There were silks for the royal household and jewelry for the fingers of the royal wives. There were gifts for every officer of the palace. . . .

He paused, while the last boxes were stacked around the shining runabout, incongruous and laughable amid the ancient magnificence.

And finally, the greatest gift in his power to bestow, a pearl of incomparable quality, a personal gift for the Navel of the Universe, which he begged humbly to present in person. . . .

Slowly he raised Lisette to her feet and walked her step by step down the empty space to the foot of the throne.

"Dear God no!" McCreary's voice was a whisper of horror and he started to his feet, but Janzoon and Guido clamped their hands on him and held him down, and Guido's voice spoke desperately in his ear.

"Not now, for pity's sake! They will cut you down and you cannot help her! Control yourself—for her sake!"

He sank back on the cushions, feeling their fingers bite into his arms, and he watched Lisette prostrate herself like a slave at the feet of the Sultan. Then he saw the brown hands lift her to her feet, unveil her and lead her to the throne beside his own, while the courtiers sighed in soft wonderment at her beauty.

He saw Rubensohn bow and walk slowly back to his place, a thin smile on his lips, his eyes bright with triumphant malice. He longed desperately to leap at him and tear him down and trample him on the pavement, but Guido and Janzoon still held him and he could not find even voice to curse his tormentor.

Then the document of concession was presented and the music began again, and with it the long procession of waiters, bearing food and drink. The jugglers came and the acrobats, and the dancers, moving like jointed dolls in the rhythms of the old mimes.

But McCreary saw none of it. He sat silent and stone-faced, filling himself with liquor and watching Lisette perched beside the peacock throne, being fed like a bird from the brown fingers of the Sultan.

When the evening was over, they hoisted him, dead drunk, onto the litter; and when they came to the ship, Guido and the little brown slave undressed him and put him to bed.

# Chapter Eleven

He woke, deathly sick. His head was hammering and his tongue was too big for his mouth. His skin was clammy and smelt of stale liquor, and the sheets were wrapped round him like a shroud. He saw that the cabin was full of sunlight and that a brown girl was sitting in his chair, watching him with wide, solemn eyes.

Then he remembered—and the memory was like a blow in the belly. He heaved himself off the bed and staggered to the bathroom, and after a while the brown girl came in and helped him to clean himself up and get shaved and bathed. Her service was simple and unquestioning. Her hands were soft, her movements were deft, and McCreary found her a small comfort in his manifold miseries.

He had hit rock bottom, and he knew it. He knew, too, that his own blind faith in the luck of the Irish had landed him there. He had tried to fight out of his own class and had ended on the mat with Rubensohn kicking his teeth and Lisette handed over, helpless, as part of the price of an oil deal. He asked himself why she had never told him what Rubensohn had in mind for her. The answer was very simple. She had known he could do nothing about it and

125

that he was liable to act like a bull-headed Irishman and get shot for his pains. Which left him where he was now, sitting on the edge of the bed in his underpants, holding his aching head and wondering what he should do next. The others would be wondering too—Rubensohn and Janzoon. They would be waiting for his reaction, judging him by it, preparing to counter it.

What would they expect? A red-eyed rebel, sour with hangover, charging in with his head down, easily subdued by another smack in the teeth. No profit in that for Lisette or for himself. He needed time to get a grip on himself and plan the gambits before he saw Rubensohn.

The brown girl helped him to dress and then he sent her to the galley for coffee and a sick man's breakfast. She answered quickly enough to his own Malay, but he was too fuddled to piece out much of her exotic island dialect.

The stewards were apparently dispensing for others than himself. They sent him a large jug of coffee, a slice of papaya and a small grilled fish with buttered toast. The sight of the food revolted him, but he forced himself to eat it, and by the time the last of the coffee was gone he began to feel better. His skin was yellow and blotchy, his eyes were like two holes burnt in a blanket. And when he tried to light a cigarette, his hands trembled as if with malaria.

He sent the girl back to the galley for more coffee and breakfast for herself. Then he sat down and tried to gather his strength. Outside he heard the clatter of the winches and the high voices of the loading crews. Miranha was at work and the first of the drilling equipment was on its way to the shore. Soon he would have to go on deck to superintend the loading of the motors and generators, and then, he thought, his real test would come.

For all the sickness in his belly and the ache in his heart, he would have to face them with a grin, make them uncertain of their victory, uneasy about his future actions.

He had one trump left—without him they couldn't get oil. Everything depended on how and when he played it.

The girl came back with his coffee and a plate of rice for herself. She squatted, native fashion, at his feet, and while she ate McCreary questioned her gently.

"What's your name, little one?"

"I am called Flame Flower, tuan."

"It's a pretty name."

"I am glad it pleases the tuan."

"You understand that you belong to me now?"

"I understand, tuan."

"Shortly I must go to work. While I am gone, you will wash my clothes, and when they are dry you will pack them with the others as I will show you. We are going away from here."

"Where are we going, tuan?"

"Back to Karang Sharo. We shall live there awhile."

She looked up at him with shining, guileless eyes.

"And I shall be the tuan's woman and care for him and . . ."

"You'll care for me, little one," said McCreary hastily, and added for himself, "and we'd better leave the rest for a later time. I've got problems enough as it is."

He drank the last of his coffee, got up, tossed his laundry into a heap and showed her his bag and how to pack it. Then he put on a pair of dark glasses to hide the worst ravages of the night and went up on deck.

Alfieri was standing by the winches, snapping orders at the deck hands. He greeted McCreary with curt distaste and turned away quickly. McCreary hoped he felt as green as he looked.

Captain Janzoon was pacing the for'ard deck. McCreary waved and shouted a greeting. Janzoon looked up with faint surprise and waved back, hesitantly. There were no other officers in sight, but a couple of the girls were squatting against the bulkhead, dipping into the same rice bowl and talking in high voices like the piping of birds.

McCreary walked over to the rail and watched the island boys standing on the bobbing pontoons and juggling the heavy slings while Miranha sat in his boat and shouted orders at them.

He looked across the dazzling water to the palace below the mountain and thought of Lisette. A moment later Rubensohn's high voice spoke at his elbow:

"You're stirring early, McCreary."

"Habit of years," said McCreary coolly. "The morning's the best part of the day."

"You enjoyed your evening?"

"Sure. It was a good night."

"The best come-all-ye of the season?" Rubensohn was baiting him cruelly, but McCreary forced a grin, thankful that his eyes were hidden behind the dark glasses.

"The best. What I saw of it, that is."

"Lisette looked beautiful, I thought."

"So did I."

"You don't disapprove of my bargain?"

"I think you're a bastard," said McCreary, without rancour. "But then I've known that all along. Besides, it's no skin off my nose. I'd had my share of her before she left."

It was a calculated crudity, but he saw no shame in it. He felt a grim satisfaction when he saw Rubensohn's recoil and watched him battle to control himself.

"You're tougher than I thought, McCreary." It was a high whisper, soft as silk.

"I have to be," said McCreary. "I'm playing in a tough school. And while we're talking business, there's the small matter of an agreement to be signed and delivered before I start work."

"I'll have it ready for you in an hour," said Rubensohn flatly.

"And before we sign it . . ."

"Yes?"

"I'd like to see your passport."

It took Rubensohn completely off guard. His head flicked back, his eyes narrowed and his reedy voice was unsteady.

"What are you driving at, McCreary?"

McCreary leaned back against the rail and smiled at him.

"I want a legal document, with a verifiable signature. So I'd like to see your passport."

For a long moment Rubensohn looked at him, then, surprisingly, he smiled.

"I'll let you see it before we sign. Anything else?"

"Yes. Janzoon has approached me with a proposition."

"What sort of a proposition?"

This, too, was news to Rubensohn, and in spite of his control he could not conceal the first shock of surprise.

"It's a double," said McCreary sardonically. "At the moment he can't make up his mind which leg he wants. Either to buy me out for cash and guarantee protection from you, or team up with me to oust you. We could probably do it, too."

Rubensohn gave him a long, speculative look.

"Then why do you tell me?"

"You're a big man, Rubensohn. I think you can do a lot for us," said McCreary deliberately. "But even big men can make mistakes that, in the end, destroy them. Your biggest mistake was to pick the wrong fellow to kick in the face. Janzoon will take it—and has—because he's scared. I'm not scared. I've got nothing to lose and a lot to gain. I've told you that before. It's time you understood it."

"You've changed a lot since that first night in Djakarta."

"I learn fast," said McCreary, with genial good humour. "The Irish are good horse copers."

Rubensohn nodded slowly and leaned against the rail,

absorbed in a new, private thought. After a moment he turned to McCreary.

"I'd feel happier if we could trust each other more."

"So would I," said McCreary. "But I don't doubt we'll come to it in time." He changed the subject abruptly. "The loading'll be finished in a couple of hours. As soon as we've got the agreement fixed, I'd like to be off. You'll be down often, of course, to watch progress?"

"Every day," said Rubensohn, "until the well blows in."

"Then you're thinking of killing me?"

"I had thought of it," said Rubensohn, with surprising frankness. "Now I've changed my mind. I'll get you to kill Janzoon instead."

"You're lying again," said McCreary amiably.

Rubensohn flushed angrily.

"Now look, McCreary . . ."

"Look yourself, me bright boyo! Why not admit it? You'd like us both out of the way so you can take the whole profit for yourself. Else why did you offer Alfieri the captain's job?"

"Did Alfieri tell you that?"

"A little bird told me."

"Have you told Janzoon?"

"I've thought about it," said McCreary carefully. "Just as I've thought about dropping a word about the island that the Sultan's new wife came from the Peacock Pavilion in Saigon, and about leaving a message for Scott Morrison that the deal is phony and that there's a dead man in Djakarta to prove it; just as I've worked out every damn trick in the book to stop you getting a drop of oil, if there's half a chance I'm going to be killed when it comes in. Now, Rubensohn, don't you think it's time you played at least one honest hand?"

And with that he turned away and walked over to the winches to watch the first generator being hoisted overside.

He didn't count too much on all his brave talk. It was a nice Irish gesture, and he hoped it might give Rubensohn a headache or two, but it was rather like old Paddy Moynighan, drunk as a lord, prancing at the crossroads and waving his shillelagh at the cows. Come close to him and he'd fetch you a crack or two, but he always ended the same way, with a broken head and a bloody nose, lying in the ditch in the morning.

Two hours later, accompanied by Guido and Agnello, the engineer officer, and Flame Flower and Agnello's girl, McCreary left the ship for the drilling site. He had the survey charts in his pocket and with them Rubensohn's contract giving him, in return for services rendered, a quarter share of the proceeds of the sale and the right to claim payment direct from the purchaser.

He had no illusions about the validity of the document. There is no law in the world that can enforce a payment to a criminal accessory. He was more interested in the fact that Rubensohn's name really was Rubensohn and that he had a specimen of his legal signature verified from the passport. The passport had given him other information, too. Rubensohn was a British subject, Polish by birth, who had been naturalized ten years before. His age was forty-eight, and his names were Joseph Ladislas. The passport itself was a double-sized book to cope with Rubensohn's peripatetic existence.

The day might come when he could make use of these facts. For the present there were other matters to occupy him.

When they came to the beach, they found Miranha waiting for them with a couple of boys to carry the bags and the radio pack. The rest of the equipment was already on its way, carried on poles and bamboo hurdles by a small brown army.

They set off along the winding track that led through

the villages of the littoral towards the low spur beyond
which lay the drilling area.

Agnello walked ahead with Miranha, and Guido and
McCreary strode along together, with the girls trotting like
excited children behind them.

The dust rose in small clouds from their feet, parching
their lips and settling in the nostrils. The broad green
leaves hung listless, and the air was crackling with insects
and the chatter of the villages.

Slowly the drink sweated out of him and McCreary
began to be absorbed in the strident, colourful life of the
huts that lined the road. Women, naked to the waist,
suckled children at the doors or stood knee-deep in the
roadside pools washing themselves and the family clothes.
A smith beat out the wavering blade of a kris over a small
charcoal fire. A vendor padded by with long bamboo poles
over his shoulders, from which hung bunches of bananas
and baskets of bean curd and brown rice. Laughing girls sat
weaving the big palm mats which would make the walls of
the houses and the beds on which they would sleep. A
water buffalo wandered by, goaded by a toddler with a
sharp bamboo stick, and a flight of swallows dipped down
from the blue sky into the shade of the pathway. High up in
the bare branches of a flame tree a boy was picking the
scarlet blooms and putting them into a basket hung round
his neck. A silversmith, old and blear-eyed, was tapping a
bowl with a tiny hammer, and beside him a boy with honey-
coloured skin and tiny hands like a woman's was whittling a
comb from soft white wood.

For a while Guido, too, was absorbed in the spectacle;
then he broached the subject that was troubling him.

"It was bad last night, *amico*."

"Very bad, Guido."

"You—you understand I had to do what I did. Otherwise they would have killed you."

"I know that, Guido. I'm grateful."

"What are you going to do now?"

"Work," said McCreary tersely. "Work and plan to get Lisette out and bring Rubensohn down."

Guido whistled.

"Get her out? You think you can?"

"I'm going to try."

"But how? You saw what the palace is like. The women are kept in their own quarters. There are guards . . ."

"I know." McCreary nodded gravely. "But we can make a beginning. These girls . . ." He pointed to the two small figures giggling behind them. "They come from the palace, remember. They know the layout. They can help."

"If they will, yes."

McCreary looked at him sharply.

"What do you mean . . . 'if'?"

Guido grinned at him like a wise goat.

"These are women, too, McCreary. They look like children, but they could be any age from fifteen to twenty-five. They have been given to the tuans—they regard themselves as our women and us as their men. It would be wise to remember that. If you want help, you will have to pay for it, one way or another. If you want your Lisette back, you must have an ally, not a rival."

"Hell!" said McCreary succinctly.

"That's what I mean," chuckled Guido. "Another thing . . ."

"Yes?"

"You get your Lisette out. It is still not enough. You have to get her away from the island, otherwise you both end in the hands of the torturers. You think Rubensohn will give you a free passage on the *Corsair*?"

"I doubt it."

"So you think of that, too. You remember that we are three people—you, me, the girl—anchored on an island, and the man who owns the transport is a man who wants to kill you."

"I've thought of it," said McCreary. "I've thought it over and over, and it all adds up to the one answer. Someday, soon, I'm going to kill Rubensohn. But before I do, I'm going to strip him of everything he's got. Don't ask me how, but I'm going to do it."

"I wish you luck," said Guido, without conviction.

"Tell me." McCreary dropped his voice and jerked his head at the pair ahead of him. "This Agnello. What sort of man is he? He's going to work with me most of the time. I'd like to think I could trust him."

Guido shrugged and kicked out at a pecking chicken.

"You know engineers. They eat cotton waste and bathe in machine oil. Sometimes I think they want nothing better than to marry an engine and breed little ones. Agnello is like that. He has a sad face like a horse, and he never says more than two words. What he thinks or feels you will have to find out for yourself. If you can make him a friend, we are much stronger. Without him, they cannot run the ship."

"I'll spend some time on him," said McCreary thoughtfully.

Now they had left the last of the villages and were rounding the low spur that divided the drilling area from the rest of the island. The track led upwards through thick jungle, and beside it a small stream tumbled downwards over green rocks overhung with ferns and the skeleton roots of breadfruit trees.

After about half an hour's tramping they came to the area itself, a wide clearing that looked eastward over the sea and the scattered islands. Behind it was the serrated spine of the mountains rising slowly to the palace itself and the humped cone behind it.

The clearing swarmed with brown, chattering men, and the equipment was piled along one side of it in neat stacks.

McCreary looked about him with a practiced eye. It was a good spot, easy to work in. There was clean mountain water, free from the pollution of the kampongs. There was good timber close, handy, and bamboo and palm boles in abundance for the lighter construction of the huts. When the day was ended, they could sit and look out over the sea, away from the plague of mosquitoes, and, if they climbed the spine of the mountains, they could look down on the approaches to the palace. Perhaps, even, he might catch a glimpse of Lisette as she walked in the walled gardens among the women. He reminded himself to ask Guido to get a pair of field glasses from the ship.

Miranha came up to him, waving his arms and hopping from foot to foot, and talking in his huckster's whine.

"Here we are, senhor. You are the number one here, they tell me. There is your gear, there are my workmen. You tell Miranha what you want and we get busy, eh?"

"Right!" said McCreary crisply, and calling to Agnello and Guido, he began pacing out the locations.

"The derrick goes here, slap in the center. Motor housings here. Machine shop and maintenance over there. You'll find all the stuff numbered on the schedule, Agnello, together with a working diagram. The crates are stencilled to correspond with the number on the list. Get yourself a team and start work. Over against the hill, facing out to sea, we'll have the living huts—two of them; next to them a storehouse for machine parts, a long, roofed shelter for the piping and the big stuff. A cook house here. The radio goes in my hut, Guido. Below the derrick, shelters for the labour crew. Over here, the fuel dumps—a thatch cover will be enough for them . . ."

For a while it was a babbling chaos, but by midafternoon they had sorted themselves out and McCreary was able to stand with Guido on the upper edge of the clearing and watch the job take shape. Agnello and his boys were working on the foundations for the big splay legs of the derrick; the logs for the engine beds were being cut and hauled in from the jungle; the frames for the living huts and the shelters were already in position, and the brown figures were swarming over the roofs, laying the thatch of alang grass.

McCreary found a deep satisfaction in this ant-like activity. He had seen it before many times, in many places, but each time it was new, because each well is a new challenge, and the day the bits bite in for the first time is like a new race for an unknown yearling, with the crowds waiting and the sleek bodies shining at the starter's gate and the silks fluttering in the small wind and no one knowing what number will go up at the finish.

It was sacrilege to think of it as a criminal enterprise, with death and disaster at the end of it.

Guido squatted on his haunches and chewed reflectively on a grass stalk. He said hesitantly, "I've been thinking, McCreary."

"What?"

Guido pointed down the hillside to where the flapping scarecrow figure of Miranha was hustling a line of boys cutting alang grass.

"There's the man who can help you. He knows this place. He knows the back doors to the palace. He's got a boat, too—that ketch moored in the main harbour. He's a trader, isn't he? He knows these waters. At least he could get you to Timor . . ."

"I don't trust him," said McCreary. "He's a dock rat. He'd sell his own mother for a fistful of coppers."

"You don't have to trust him," Guido persisted. "You only have to frighten him."

"And how would I do that?"

"Simple enough. When this thing blows up, as it must do one day, like a bomb, who is here? Not us, not Rubensohn—Miranha! If the Sultan wants to roast somebody's toes, who's the nearest? Who's the interpreter and the agent? Miranha! I think if you talk to him someday and tell him the facts and offer him a nice fat reward, you will have yourself an ally—and a boat as well."

McCreary looked down at the little Neapolitan and laughed.

"We'd better change jobs, Guido. Seems you're the only one with brains around here."

"Not me!" said Guido firmly. "Not for a million pounds would I sleep in your bed! Every night I would have nightmares, thinking my throat was cut."

"I've got 'em now," said McCreary somberly. "But somehow I've got to learn to live with 'em."

# Chapter Twelve

By sunset, the living huts and the main storehouses had been built. The base frame for the derrick was in place; the teak logs had been stripped and laid out near the engine positions. Miranha had marshalled his workers and checked their tools back into storage and herded them homewards. Guido had gone with him, after setting up the radio pack and giving McCreary detailed instructions for its operation. They had arranged a morning schedule, when Guido would call McCreary and give him half an hour's practice on the key, passing on at the same time any news from the ship.

Guido had wanted to stay the night, but McCreary had refused. It would be unwise, so soon, to let Rubensohn see too close an association between himself and the little radioman. Their communication system was sketchy enough, and at all costs it had to be kept open.

The huts were modest but habitable. Each had two bunks framed with bamboo and covered with palm matting. There was a rough table and a couple of bamboo chairs, knocked together at astonishing speed by Miranha's workmen. For the rest, they were furnished from the ship with clean bedcovers and eating utensils and mosquito netting and a basic stock of first-aid gear, suppressant tablets and liquor—half a dozen cases of beer and two bottles of whisky per man. Their food would be tinned stores supplemented by local produce supplied under contract by Miranha.

McCreary and Agnello were sitting together outside McCreary's hut, drinking beer and looking down over the jungle fringe to the luminous water of the small bay between the two spurs of cliff. Twenty yards away the two girls were giggling over the cook fires, from which rose the pungent, exotic flavour of native cooking. This would be the first meal they would serve to their new masters, and the girls were making it an elaborate production.

They sipped their beer and smoked contentedly, saying little.

The horse-faced engineer had a quality of relaxation that contrasted sharply with the bubbling temperament of Guido. He talked sparsely, a man content with his own company, and his simple, pragmatic phrases carried their own quiet conviction. McCreary found him a satisfying companion for the long evening hours when he, too, was busy with his own thoughts.

They were halfway through their second bottle of beer when Agnello said calmly, "I like this. It satisfies me."

"What—the beer?" McCreary was miles away—up the mountain with Lisette.

"No. This work. To see something building under your hands. To make a hole in the ground and see good oil come out of it. I am an engineer. I have great respect for oil."

"So have lots of other people," said McCreary, with offhand irony.

"No. They see it as a commodity, a source of profit. An engineer sees it as a source of life to the things he loves most in the world—good engines turning sweetly on their bearings."

"It's a good thought," said McCreary. "Better than many I've heard lately. Tell me, Agnello, how did you come to join this outfit? Why do you stay with it?"

Agnello puffed placidly at his pipe and considered the question.

"Simple enough. Here I am number one. On a big ship I would be number two. Nobody bothers me and I get good pay. That's important. In Florence I have a wife and two daughters who must soon be provided with dowries. So it suits me."

"Lucky fellow."

Agnello smoked his pipe and sipped his beer and looked out into the moonrise. For all his horse face and his melancholy eyes, McCreary thought he must be a singularly happy man. His next question brought a smile to McCreary's lips. Agnello coughed and fidgeted and jerked his thumb in the direction of the girls at the cook fires.

He said awkwardly, "What—what am I expected to do with that?"

McCreary chuckled.

"It depends on you, Agnello."

Agnello frowned and mumbled unhappily.

"I know, but—but I am not interested. When I was younger, I was happy to make a fool of myself. Now, when I see my friends going down to the houses near the docks, when I see things happen like last night in the palace, I think of my daughters, and I have no taste left for it. I just ask. I don't want to criticize what you do, but for me . . ."

McCreary dropped his cigarette on the ground and trod it out with his heel. He grinned wryly in the darkness and said, "It's fine with me, Agnello. So long as you're here, we'll share my hut. You'll keep me out of mischief, too. The girls can bunk in together."

For the first time a slow smile dawned on the engineer's long face. He said gratefully, "A thousand thanks, my friend. Now I can enjoy my supper."

Then they both laughed, and McCreary thought that he, too, might eat better and sleep sounder, and build a little hope on a new ally.

The girls brought out one of the tables from the huts and laid on it dishes of steaming rice and curried fish surrounded by smaller masses of spices and side meats, cradled in green leaves. Then they squatted on the grass and watched the men pick gingerly through the unfamiliar dishes and finally settle down to enjoy them.

They giggled self-consciously when McCreary praised the meal and dismissed them to their own supper.

Flame Flower hesitated a moment and asked, "When do I come to the tuan?"

"Not tonight," said McCreary gently. "When I send for you. Tonight I have things to talk about with my friend."

"All night?" The childish eyes widened with disbelief.

McCreary grinned and patted her sleek, perfumed hair.

"No. Not all night. But we are tired. Tomorrow we work early. We need sleep."

The girl nodded and her small brown face split into a flashing smile. This she could understand. So long as she pleased the tuan, there would always be tomorrow and the nights after. The real shame was when a woman lacked the power to attract a man, and she was very anxious to attract this lean fellow with the soft voice and the laughing eyes.

She turned away to join her companion and, a long time later, while Agnello snored contentedly, McCreary could hear their twittering voices from the farther hut. They reminded him of Lisette penned with all the other alien women in the fretwork palace on the hill. The thought of her was an ache in his heart and a sharp torment in his flesh.

Early next morning, when Agnello was out with Miranha and the labour gangs, Guido sent him word on the buzzer.

"Rubensohn's on his way up to see you. He's given me a radio message for Morrison."

"What is it?" signalled McCreary awkwardly. It was a long time since he had worked a key and his fingers were slow and his groups uncertain.

"Test begins . . . Operations begun stop. Expect early result stop. Stand by further reports stop . . . Message ends. I sent it."

"O.K.! Any more news?"

"Argument Janzoon-Alfieri still in progress. Subject *Corsair* command. More when I see you. Palace courier arrived first light with message for Rubensohn. End news."

"Thanks. Remember field glasses."

"Will bring this afternoon. Practice sending. Hard to read."

McCreary spelt out: "Go to hell!" then switched off the power, laid aside the headphones and lit a cigarette. He was smiling to himself. His talk with Rubensohn was beginning to have effect. To cover his own maneuvers, Rubensohn must have talked with Janzoon and given him a doctored version of Alfieri's ambitions. It was part of his technique, to muddy up the water and make profit from the confusion of his subordinates.

Well, McCreary had stirred some mud of his own, and like a cranky Celt, he found a deal of pleasure in it. He stepped out into the raw sunshine, called Flame Flower to tidy his hut, then walked down the slope to the work gangs, whistling jauntily to himself.

It was an old tune this morning, called in Kerry "The Hounds of Glenloe." It told of the hunt slavering up hill and down dale while the canny old fox sat in his earth and thumbed his nose at the lot of them. For a long time now McCreary had had great sympathy with Brother Fox.

Miranha was directing a bunch of boys stacking the big fuel drums under a thatched shelter. When McCreary came up to him, he showed his teeth in a betel-stained smile and immediately launched into a rasping monologue.

"We're doing well, senhor, aren't we? See! It begins to

look like something. But you've got to understand these fellows. Smile at 'em, but keep driving all the time. You're satisfied, I hope. If there's anything you want, tell Miranha. I get it fixed, pronto. I promised Mr. Rubensohn cooperation, fullest service. When I say that, I mean it. Value for money, eh? That makes good business for both of us."

"Sure," said McCreary coolly. "You're doing fine. Just keep the work rolling. I'll let you know if there's anything I want."

Miranha licked his lips. His bloodshot eyes looked both ways at once. He said in a confidential whisper:

"You—er . . . you couldn't sell me a bottle of whisky, senhor? This native toddy ruins a man. I'm prepared to pay . . ."

"I'll give you a bottle," said McCreary curtly.

Miranha began to pour out a profuse speech of gratitude, but McCreary cut him short.

"Tell me, what are you getting paid for this?"

"Three pounds sterling a day, in Indonesian rupiahs. It's only a pittance, of course, but . . ."

"But it's more than you'd earn otherwise, and you get a cut from the boys' wages and a profit on any materials you supply and on the food rations. . . ."

Miranha shrugged and spread his hands in deprecation.

"Oh, a little here and there. But that's normal trade, eh? That's what I am after all—a trader. This job keeps me from my normal trips. I'm entitled to a small profit. Isn't that right?"

McCreary grinned at him ironically.

"Don't ask me, Miranha. Your contract's with Rubensohn. I just work here." He brought out a packet of cigarettes and handed one to Miranha. "Tell me, where do you trade normally?"

Miranha puffed out a cloud of smoke and talked as offhandedly as a merchant prince.

"Oh, Ambon, Buru, east to Kai Ketjil and south to Timor Laut and Timor."

"What sort of trade?"

"Foodstuffs, spices, trade cloth, normal things—it's mostly barter here. A few stones sometimes, gold and silverware. There's a small market in Dili for European export. Sometimes a girl or two, to keep the Sultan happy. You know how it goes."

"Sure," said McCreary.

"Maybe . . ." Miranha hesitated. "Maybe you do a little trade yourself sometimes?"

"A little." McCreary cocked a quizzical eyebrow. "You know how it goes?"

"I could put some business in your way, perhaps?"

"What did you have in mind?"

"This stuff." Miranha jerked his thumb at the stacks of fuel drums. "It costs like gold in Dili, which is the only place I can buy it. Then I can't build up a store because it cuts down my cargo space. So half my trip I run the ketch on sail. That doubles my time and halves my profit. You got more than you need there. I can make you a nice offer. Stone, some jade, nice pieces, and other things. If you're interested, I'll show you."

"Bring 'em up to the hut one evening. We'll talk about it."

Miranha showed his stained teeth in a wide and understanding grin.

"Good, good! I think you'll like what I show you. And we keep it private, eh? Another thing. If you want a girl any time."

"I've got a girl," said McCreary bluntly, "and she's more than I can handle. Now, jump to it! I want this stuff stacked in the next twenty minutes. Then you can start on the steel sections."

"Yes, senhor." Miranha flapped away, cursing the

Malays in fluent and obscene dialect, and McCreary looked after him with sardonic satisfaction.

Then he saw Rubensohn coming into the clearing, riding like a rajah on a litter carried by six men. He was dressed in a tussah suit and a white panama and was smoking one of his long cigars.

They lowered the litter and he stepped out awkwardly, then stood a moment looking round the clearing, measuring the progress with a critical eye. McCreary tossed away his cigarette and walked over to him. Rubensohn greeted him cheerfully.

"This is what I like to see, McCreary! Good organization, fast work. You've got everything you want?"

"For the present, yes."

"When do you think you can spud in?"

"Early to say. But we'll be ready in a week at the outside. Six days maybe."

"Good. You're satisfied with Miranha?"

"So far, yes."

"You've got all the labour you want?"

"Yes."

"One thing, McCreary. I'm sorry about it, but I'll have to take Agnello away from you for a couple of days."

"Why?"

Rubensohn shrugged and waved his cigar.

"A message from the palace. We made the Sultan a present of some mechanical equipment: a lighting plant for one thing, an automobile . . . He wants them put into running order. The lighting's the biggest job—lots of wiring to be run and . . ."

"You can't have Agnello!" said McCreary.

Rubensohn frowned.

"You don't understand, McCreary. This is . . ."

"I understand damn well!" McCreary was curt and determined. "You gave me a free hand here. You see the stage we're at. If I don't have Agnello, I can't get this gear running on time. It's as simple as that."

Rubensohn was apologetic.

"I'm sorry, McCreary, but you know the way things are run here. The Sultan is the Navel of the Universe—first cousin to God Almighty. I can't refuse him. He could shut us down with a twitch of his finger."

McCreary thought about it for a moment. The point was clear enough, but if anyone were going to the palace, it should be someone who could make a profit out of it for Lisette and for himself.

He said, irritably, "Why waste a good engineer on a simple job like that? Any electrician's apprentice could do it. Why not leave me Agnello and sent Guido instead? He's a radioman—he could run the wiring and connect it to the generator. He can drive a car, surely. Damn it all, Rubensohn, let's be sensible about this thing! I don't give a curse whether the Sultan goes to bed by candlelight for the rest of his life, but we both care if this rig isn't working on schedule. I want Agnello here!"

Rubensohn was obviously glad of the suggestion. He said heartily, "Of course! Wonder I didn't think of it myself. Guido's the obvious man. I'll send him up there this afternoon."

"Leave it till the morning," said McCreary. "I've got him coming over here this afternoon. My radio isn't satisfactory. I want him to have a look at it."

Rubensohn chuckled shrilly and patted him on the shoulder.

"You're a prickly fellow, McCreary. But I like the way you work. It gives me great confidence for the future."

"I'm sure it does," said McCreary sourly. "Now, if you want to look around, I can give you ten minutes. Agnello doesn't know enough Malay and I've got to teach a dozen of these boys how to handle and bolt the derrick sections."

But Rubensohn was not to be shaken off so easily. Even

after McCreary had left him to begin work on the steel frame of the derrick, he strolled about the clearing watching the work with shrewd, appraising eyes. McCreary began to be afraid that he would not leave before Guido arrived and that he would lose this first, slender chance of communicating with Lisette.

Just before noon, however, Rubensohn began to show signs of tiring. His tussah suit was staining under the armpits and his pale face was streaming with sweat. He sat down on a log and mopped his cheeks and tried to smoke another cigar. Then, abruptly, he surrendered. He signalled to the litter bearers, shouted farewell to McCreary and left, a crumpled white figure swaying down the hillside and into the jungle overhang.

McCreary climbed down from the framework and called to Agnello to join him.

"Let's have a beer, Agnello."

"As you like. But it's not noon yet."

"The boys are doing all right. We can leave them to it. I want to talk to you."

Together they climbed the small slope to the living huts and went, gratefully, into the shade, which smelt of leaves and fresh grass and the lingering musky perfume of Flame Flower.

McCreary brought out the beer. They toasted each other, then sank the first glasses in a long, thirsty gulp.

"Another one, Agnello?"

"Thanks. It goes down easily."

This time they sipped it slowly, tasting it with relish.

McCreary said blandly, "I've got things to tell you, Agnello—a long story."

Agnello nodded.

"You woke me last night, shouting in your sleep."

"Did I say much?"

"Enough."

"Right! I'll tell you the rest of it. When I've finished,

I'm going to put it up to you to help me. I'll understand if you refuse, but I must count on your secrecy."

"You can count on it," said Agnello, in his grave, practical voice.

McCreary told him.

When he had finished, Agnello's face was longer than ever and his limpid eyes were angry. He said simply, "A dirty business. And to sell a woman like that is the dirtiest of all. I have daughters—good girls. I feel that part most."

"Will you help me then?"

"I'll help, if I can. What do you want?"

McCreary told him about the Sultan's summons and how he had persuaded Rubensohn to send Guido. Then he went on:

"I have the idea that Guido may be able to make contact with Lisette. At least he'll be able to get some idea of the layout of the palace and of the women's quarters in particular. When he comes this afternoon, I'm going to take him up the mountain there and see what sort of a view we get from this side. I may want to spend more and more time up there over the next few days. Can you run the camp and keep the work going? And answer any questions of Rubensohn if he comes when I'm not here?"

"No trouble at all," said Agnello. "But you must think further than that."

"I know," said McCreary. "But I can't think too far yet. I've got to play the cards as they fall. The big problem is to lift ourselves off the island once I get Lisette out."

Agnello put down his beer and began filling his pipe with maddening deliberation. Then he said calmly, "Miranha's got a boat."

"I can't trust all this to Miranha."

"You don't have to do that. You tell me he wants you to sell him fuel. Good. You point out to him that you can't do it openly or all at once. You suggest he move his ketch out of the main harbour and down to the bay there, so you can let him have a drum now and others later. He can take the stuff down at night. He will stay there so long as there's a chance of getting more out of you. So you have your boat, fuelled and ready to move, whenever you want."

McCreary whistled softly.

"Holy Patrick! It might work at that! And if I were to get myself one of these native dugouts and interest myself in some night fishing, so they'd be used to seeing me around . . . Let's have another drink to celebrate a noble thought."

"Not for me," said Agnello, with his slow smile. "I'll walk down and see how the work goes. These boys are intelligent—but they are like the southerners in my country. They would rather sing and sun themselves than do an honest day's work."

McCreary watched him walk slowly down to the derrick site, puffing his pipe, a picture of guileless contentment, the man who ran the engines while the passengers drank and seduced each other's wives and the captain took coffee with the owner's representative.

He turned back into the hut, took out a pencil and paper and began to sketch a plan of campaign.

The little brown girl came in and squatted down at his feet, watching him with expectant eyes. McCreary stroked her head absently and she leaned against him, purring like a contented kitten.

It took him twenty minutes to realize that here was yet another ally, perhaps the strongest of all.

He leaned down and lifted her, feather-light, and sat her on the table in front of him. She sat there, smiling like a small brown doll, perfect as a doll, with her small, pointed breasts and the honey skin and her tiny expressive hands.

He asked her gently, "What did you do in the palace, small one?"

"I served the Sultan's women. Sometimes, when one of the others was sick, I danced in the *djoged* dances."

"Were you shut in, like the Sultan's women?"

She laughed, amused at his ignorance.

"No! Only the wives and the concubines were kept like that. We others were free to come and go. We were neither married nor betrothed nor concubines."

"What would have happened to you if you had not come to me?"

She pouted and shrugged indifferently.

"One of the servants might have asked to marry me. The Sultan might have given me as a gift to one of the court. We were his property, to keep or give away."

"Were you born in the palace?"

"No. I was born in the town. But my parents gave me to the palace, because they were too poor to pay the Sultan's tax."

"What do the women do—the Sultan's women?"

"They sit and talk. They listen to the musicians beyond the screens. They eat sweetmeats and sew and have babies. Sometimes they walk in their own garden, in the cool."

"And no man comes near them—only the Sultan?"

"No man. There are guards on the doors and it is death to any man to enter."

"Do they never have lovers then?"

Her eyes widened with surprise and a hint of fear.

"Oh, no! Who would risk the torturers and the fiery death?"

"What do you mean?"

She told him, making a pantomime with her small, fluent hands.

"If a woman were unfaithful to the Sultan, she and her lover would be tortured first, under each other's eyes. Then they would be bound and thrown together into Gurung Merapi, the mountain of fire."

A grim prospect, thought McCreary. Enough to cool the ardour of lovers. He thought of Lisette penned among the twittering, idle concubines, eating her heart out in the walled garden, and he was filled with anger against Rubensohn for what he had done to her. Flame Flower watched him with puzzled, questioning eyes. He took out a cigarette and stuck it between his lips. When he made to light it, the girl took the lighter from his hands and laughed with delight when finally she snapped it into flame. He smoked a few moments in silence, wondering how to frame the next question. He reminded himself of Guido's warning that this, too, was a woman—apt to jealousy and subtle revenge. Then he hit on an idea.

He said carefully, "The woman who was given to the Sultan was my sister."

To his surprise, Flame Flower laughed happily and clapped her hands.

"Then you are both fortunate. To be the Sultan's woman is a great honour."

"No!" said McCreary gravely. "I am lonely for her. We were like flowers on the same stem, beans in the same pod. She did not want to go. She wanted to marry one of her own kind. I wanted her to be near me when I, too, married my woman. Can you understand that?"

"Yes. Sometimes there were women who did not wish to come into the palace. They were sad and wept often—but only when the Sultan was not there."

"I want to get a message to my sister," said McCreary carefully, "and have her send a message to me. If I knew she was happy, I could be happy, too. Do you know how I could send it?"

"I could take it for you."

"You could?"

"Of course. That is how news comes and goes in the palace. We belong there. We can go back at any time. The guards know us and let us pass freely."

"Well, I'll be damned!" said McCreary, in English. "As simple as that."

"And when you know she is happy," said Flame Flower, guilelessly, "you will begin to be happy with me?"

Then he knew it wasn't simple at all. It was damnably complicated. If he didn't watch his step with this girl, he'd be getting poison in his rice bowl and Lisette might well fall into the hands of the Sultan's executioner.

# Chapter Thirteen

"What do you make of it, Guido?"

"Narrow," said Guido cryptically. "Narrow like the beam of a ship. When you look at it from the front it spreads lengthwise all along the flank of the hill. But from here, end on, it has no depth. The hill is like a cliff behind it and the plateau is narrow. It is the gardens that make the illusion."

They were lying on their bellies, high up in the neck of the re-entrant above the drilling side and looking southward along the flank of the hill to the Sultan's palace. Below them lay the jungle fringe and above them the sparser vegetation of the heights. Two big boulders hid them from view and the binoculars brought the building almost to finger-touch.

"What else, Guido?"

"There is a colonnade at this end and the garden has a fountain in it, half hidden by trees. No . . . wait! This garden is completely enclosed. It does not join the hanging gardens in front!"

"Can you see anybody?"

"No. It's full of shadows."

McCreary looked at his watch.

"It's three o'clock! Flame Flower said they came out to walk in the cool."

"But this may not be their garden."

"It's got to be!" said McCreary desperately. "It's on the same side of the palace as the screen we saw. It's closed off from the other gardens. It must be!"

"Here, look for yourself!"

Guido handed him the glasses, then hoisted himself up against the rock and lit a cigarette. McCreary focussed again and scanned the dappled garden behind the high wall and the elaborate colonnade at the end of it. The fountain was playing gently, but, unless they were hidden by the trees, there were no women in the garden. They would show up quickly enough in their bright clothes. Perhaps if he waited awhile, they would come. The afternoon was still young.

He shifted his position and began to scan the green sloping hillside that lay between their observation post and the boundaries of the palace.

When the time came to bring Lisette out, this would be the way they would have to come—along the hillside and over the secondary hills and down the re-entrant to the drilling site. The normal approach would be closed to them by the guards and the milling villagers.

Carefully, he swept the hillside, up and down, along the jungle fringe, higher up in the sparse savannah towards the saddle. There was no path. The green carpet was unbroken. It was as if by custom or interdict this approach to the palace was barred to the population of Karang Sharo.

McCreary put down the glasses and rubbed his eyes.

"Nothing yet. We'll wait awhile longer."

"Relax a moment, *amico*, and tell me what you want me to do tomorrow."

McCreary propped his back against a shaded rock and began to give his instructions. They were crisp and detailed. He had thought them out carefully.

"First, you're going up to the palace in the morning to install a lighting plant. It isn't very big, so it won't light the whole palace. My guess—which could be wrong—is that you'll be instructed to light the Sultan's apartments. My hope is that you may be asked to extend it to the women's quarters. Even if you're not, you'll be moving about the palace. You'll have to find an outside location for the motor first, then you'll have to work out a wiring plan. That gives you an excuse to use a pencil and paper and draw me some plans—exits, entrances, positions of guards, and, most important of all, the various approaches to the women's quarters. If you can work in a master switch somewhere accessible, that might help, too. Are you clear so far?"

"Like crystals," said Guido cheerfully.

"How much Malay do you know?"

"Oh . . . sailorman's needs. You know—money, food, liquor . . ."

"And women!"

"Clever fellow," said Guido genially. "How did you guess?"

"My grandmother had second sight," said McCreary. "It's a pity you're so damned ignorant, otherwise you'd be able to find out a lot from chatting to the servants or the vizier or whoever's showing you around."

"Leave it to me, *compar'*. I might surprise you."

"I hope so. Now listen, Guido, this is the most important part of all. I don't know what hope you've got of making contact with Lisette—precious little, probably. You can't risk passing a note. You can't risk a direct approach even if you do catch sight of her. But, somehow, you've got to try to tell her that we're planning to get her out, that this side of the palace is where she must watch and that when she gets a message from me—no matter how—she's to act on it without question."

"I'll sing it to her," said Guido, with heavy irony.

"That's just what you will do," said McCreary sharply.

"And for God's sake sing it in English, not Neapolitan. Even the Pope of Rome can't understand that!"

"You offend me, *amico!* Neapolitan is the language of lovers. Even my girl is beginning to learn it. And talking of lovers, you didn't give me time to tell you of our lovers on the *Corsair.*"

"Who's that?"

"Janzoon and Alfieri!" Guido leaned back against the rock face and laughed happily. "*Mamma mia,* what a spectacle! It started the moment Rubensohn left the ship. My cabin is near the bridge. I hear Janzoon call for Alfieri over the speakers. When he comes, Janzoon tells him he had word from the owner that Alfieri had asked for the captain's post when Janzoon retires. Alfieri splutters and denies it. He would like to call the owner a liar, but he doesn't dare. Janzoon strips him down like a banana, gives him extra duties and cancels his shore leave and tells him he will write him in the log. All the time Alfieri looks down his Venetian nose and snuffles, because he doesn't know whose bed he's in and who pays at the end of it. Oh, and another thing . . ."

"Yes?"

"Janzoon gave me a message for you. He's coming ashore in the morning. He'll be paying you a little visit."

"Now, I wonder . . ." chuckled McCreary, ". . . I wonder why he'd want to do that."

He slewed himself round again and focussed the glasses on the palace garden. At its lowest point the wall looked anything from ten to twelve feet high; at its highest there was a drop of fifty feet to the jungle trees. A man would need rope and a grappling hook to scale it. It would be simpler to get out than to get in. There was a big tree near the lower corner and its branches were thick and hung low to the level of the garden. Suddenly his eye was caught by a flash of colour in the shadows of the colonnade. He lost it for a moment, then it appeared again and two figures in bright sarongs and blouses appeared and walked hand in hand towards the fountain.

McCreary handed the glasses to Guido and said sharply, "Look at 'em, Guido, and tell me—men or women? They all look the same at this distance."

"Not to me, *amico!*" said Guido, with a connoisseur's conviction. "Let me see . . . No, they're women. There are two more coming out, but neither of them is Lisette."

"We're right!" said McCreary excitedly. "That's the women's quarters and the women's garden. Now we know where to look for her!"

But though they waited and waited, taking turns with the glasses, they could not find Lisette among the bright, bird-like women walking in the dappled shade. After a long time they gave it up and walked slowly down through the jungle to the drilling site.

The Sharo boys were still scurrying, ant-like, through the clearing, and the steel skeleton of the derrick was rising like a giant spider web against the peach-coloured sky.

That night, after they had eaten, Miranha came to see him.

Agnello winked solemnly at McCreary and walked out to smoke his pipe. The two girls crept into the hut and sat on the bed, curious as children, while Miranha spread his offerings on the table under the kerosine lamp.

The first was a wash-leather bag of river diamonds, rough and lifeless, which Miranha spilled out on the table. McCreary looked at them with concealed interest. A lapidary could have guessed at their value, but to McCreary they might have been a handful of pebbles. There were other stones, emeralds and rubies, cut cabochon fashion and set in the flimsy filigree of the native craftsmen. There were two small jade figures, exquisitely carved, a set of Indian ivories representing the manifestations of Siva, a clutter of carved ornaments of fine workmanship and a pair of jewelled daggers.

McCreary turned them over in his hands, stirred by their odd, exotic beauty, yet careful to conceal his interest from the huckster's eyes of Miranha.

He said indifferently, "What are they worth?"

Miranha waved a dirty hand and gave him a gap-toothed smile.

"More to you than to me. You see I'm honest with you. My best market is in Dili. There they offer me perhaps a tenth of their value and I have to take it. But you, when you go away you have a chance for a big profit. It's good stuff. You can see that."

"What's it worth to you, now?"

"Say, three hundred gallons? Thirty drums?"

"Three hundred!" McCreary laughed in his face and pushed the stuff back across the table. "What do you take me for, Miranha?"

"Say twenty drums?"

"Say fifteen and we might do business. I say 'might'"— McCreary held up a warning finger—"because there's a risk in this. If Rubensohn found out, I'm in the fire and so are you. I lose my job, you lose your profit and your fuel. Those are ten-gallon drums. How do you expect to get 'em away without being seen? You can't just roll 'em down to the beach under Rubensohn's nose."

"I could come at night and siphon it out."

"To hell with that! Once we start drilling, God knows who's likely to be here at night. No, if you want the stuff, we'll do it this way. Run your ketch out of the main harbour and anchor her in the cove down there. Then you can come up at night and take a couple of drums at a time. Not all in one week either. Any fool with half an eye could see if they all went off at once. Spread 'em over a month or six weeks, and nobody will be any wiser. We're going to be running our motors day and night during the drilling time, and I want this to look like normal usage."

Miranha looked unhappy and tried to haggle.

"Fifteen drums—a hundred and fifty gallons . . . it's too little for what I pay."

McCreary waved him away.

"It's no worry to me, Miranha. You opened the deal. Take it or leave it."

"Maybe . . . maybe for another bottle of whisky . . . ?"

"I'll throw in the whisky because I'm Irish and generous. Is that settled?"

"I'm being robbed," said Miranha unhappily. "But all the same . . ."

"You're doing damn well and you know it," said McCreary with a grin. "Half the stuff is junk and the other half will cost me boot leather and commission trying to . . ."

There was a noise like an express train and the ground rocked crazily under their feet. The girls screamed and the lamp swung high against the ceiling thatch and back again. Then the noise passed and the ground steadied again and they looked at each other with wide, startled eyes.

"Earth tremor," said Miranha uneasily. "We get them sometimes. We are in the belt. But that was a big fellow. Sometimes . . ." He licked his lips and gestured towards the rear wall of the hut. "Sometimes I wonder if Gurung Merapi isn't going to wake up and blow the lot of us to hell. He's been sleeping a long time now."

"Happy thought!" said McCreary laconically. He walked to the doorway and called out into the darkness: "Hey, Agnello! Are you all right?"

Agnello's voice floated up from the derrick site.

"I'm all right! The framework looks all right, too. I'll check it in the morning. No other damage."

A good engineer, thought McCreary wryly. He thinks of his engines like he thinks of his children.

He turned back to the hut to gather up Miranha's trinkets and hand over the bottle of whisky.

"Tomorrow," said Miranha anxiously. "Tomorrow night I run the boat round the point, then I can start to collect, eh?"

"That's right. But spread it out, remember. The longer you take, the better I'll like it."

"And if you strike oil, maybe you make me a better deal, eh?"

"If I strike oil," said McCreary genially, "I'll give you the lot. Every damned drum of it!"

He thrust the whisky into Miranha's arms and hustled him out of the hut. Then he sat down at the table and began turning over the stones and the trinkets and fingering the soft, cool surface of the jade. The two girls came peering over his shoulder and whispering excitedly.

He handed them each a small golden brooch, then patted them on their small round rumps and packed them off to bed. It was one way of keeping them happy, but he'd need to be richer than he was now to go on doing it.

He wrapped the rest of the stuff in a soiled shirt and shoved it in his bag; then he walked out into the soft moonlight to smoke a last cigarette with Agnello.

They paced slowly round the clearing, checking for signs of damage by the tremor, but they found none. As they walked, McCreary gave Agnello a terse commentary of the day's doings.

When he had finished, the engineer summed up soberly.

"So far, it is all profit. You have two possibilities of communication within the palace—Guido and your girl. You have a boat, fuelled and ready, to take you off the island. You have two allies—me and Guido; three if you count Flame Flower. You have a small stake in saleable stones to start yourself somewhere. You know what I should do now in your shoes?"

"What?"

"Get out!" said Agnello stolidly. "Plan swiftly and

surely, take your girl and leave the island. Forget the oil. Forget Rubensohn. Think only of your safety and a new start." He pointed with the stem of his pipe towards the cone of Gurung Merapi, whose smoky glow seemed angrier now, after the tremor. "Look, if you want a warning, you have it there. You are sitting on top of a volcano. Get off, before it blows up!"

"No!" said McCreary grimly. "I want Rubensohn. I want him pulled down and stripped to what he really is, and I want to take everything he's got."

"Why?" The long, comical face was somber and puzzled.

"Now that," said McCreary with a smile, "that would be the jackpot question, wouldn't it? I'm not sure that I know the answer, but I think it goes something like this. There are a million women in the world that you could bed with, breed children by and live with in moderate contentment. But there's only one who's so right and perfect for you that all the others are stale and tasteless. There are twenty million bastards in the world, too, any one of whom you'd be happy to kick in the teeth. But there's always the number one, the biggest of 'em all. Whatever he does, it's twice as bad to you, you hate him twice as much, you want him twice as dead and hurt a dozen times over. Probably," McCreary conceded ruefully, "because he's so very like your own secret image that you can't bear the sight of him. I wouldn't be knowing that either. But that's the way I am with Rubensohn. If I pull out now—even with Lisette— Rubensohn goes on in his sweet way, untouched, untouch-able; while we wander the world like a pair of fugitives. There's a murder charge against me in Djakarta—and that means in three thousand islands between New Guinea and Singapore. My girl's been sold for a scrap of paper, so that Rubensohn can clean up a few million. I'm not going to let him get away with it. I can't. And that, Agnello, me boy, is the longest damn speech I've ever made, and I'm still not sure there's sense in it at all."

Agnello sucked his pipe and pondered silently. But if he found an answer, he had no time to deliver it. The roaring came again and the ground shook under their feet, and the frightened girls rushed screaming from the hut and down the slope towards them.

When the silence came and the earth was still again, Agnello looked up at the angry mountain and said softly, "Someday it will all blow up. I pray that I am not here to see it."

# Chapter Fourteen

The next day was unbearably long.

The Sharo boys came at daybreak and they marshalled them swiftly to work on the derrick itself, strengthening the foundations against further tremors, building up the steel sections into a tall, tapering cone. McCreary and Agnello worked on the engine beds, trenching the big logs solidly in the earth and bolting the blocks hard into the flat ax grooves.

Rubensohn came in midmorning, sweating and anxious over the effects of the tremor. They gave him scant courtesy and had him on his way in half an hour.

Miranha, red-eyed and dishevelled, with a bottle of whisky under his belt, shambled among the gangs, cursing them to greater activity, while the boys sang softly and grinned at him behind their hands.

McCreary worked with merciless intensity, trying to keep his mind off Lisette and wondering at every moment what Guido was doing in the palace. At midday he drank a bottle of beer and ate a slice of papaya and was back again in twenty minutes, scrambling up the ribs of the derrick to check the work of the Sharo boys.

At three in the afternoon Captain Janzoon came to see him.

McCreary led him over to the fringe of a clearing, sat down on a log and offered cigarettes. Janzoon was red in the face and dripping with perspiration. His spade beard jerked nervously and his thick voice stumbled over the preamble.

"The proposition, McCreary—I thought about it, as I promised. I think . . . I know . . . we can do business."

"You do now," said McCreary dryly. "And what's your offer?"

"We join forces," said Janzoon eagerly. "We work together, get rid of Rubensohn and split fifty-fifty. That was your own idea, remember?"

McCreary threw back his head and laughed. Janzoon looked at him, angry and puzzled, while the startled birds squawked in the branches of the big casuarina tree behind them.

"If there is a joke, why not tell me?"

"The joke's on you, Janzoon."

"Why?"

"Rubensohn's asked me to team up with him and get rid of you."

Janzoon's jaw dropped slackly and his eyes were frightened. For a big man, with a captain's braid on his arm, there was very little fight in him.

He said unsteadily, "You—you mean that?"

"I mean it," said McCreary coolly. "He asked me to kill you. He thought Alfieri could run the ship for him and he and I could take over your share."

"But . . . but you don't believe that? You know what he's trying to do, don't you? Play us both off. Make us destroy each other!"

"I knew that, too." McCreary's voice was bitter. "So, I'm better able to look after myself. I'm going my own way, and be damned to the pair of you."

"But listen, McCreary!" Janzoon's ham fist caught at his sleeve.

McCreary brushed it aside and faced him. His eyes were hard and his crooked mouth was tight.

"You listen to me, Janzoon. Two days ago you could have had yourself a deal. Now, no. You knew what was going to happen to Lisette, but you never told me. You didn't lift hand or voice to stop it. You walked her into that palace with Rubensohn and watched her handed over as blood money. And you're still trying to squeeze a profit out of it! Well, go ahead! I wish you luck! But you'll be working on your own. And the joke is that you'll never know who's going to pull the trigger—me or Rubensohn. Now get to hell out of my camp. We're busy."

McCreary stood and watched him stumbling across the clearing, a big bull of a man with itchy fingers and a coward's heart. He felt no pity for him. He could not even bring himself to make use of him. He was sick of the backstairs whispers and the huckster's chaffering. He was spoiling for a fight—knock-down, drag-out and come again; and the sooner he could start drilling, the sooner he was likely to get it. He tossed away his cigarette and walked down to the right, where Agnello was wrestling a compressor unit over the bolt holes.

By sunset, the main frame of the derrick was completed and the machines were bedded down. It was fast going and they were pleased with themselves. McCreary yelled to the girls to bring clean clothes, and they walked down to the stream to bathe themselves and freshen up for dinner. They stood under the overhang of a small waterfall and let the cool water sluice over their bodies while the girls sat on the bank and watched them and made comments in the local dialect.

Then, dried and dressed, they tossed their soiled clothes to the girls and left them washing and scrubbing them against the smooth stones. As they emerged from the screen of bushes, they saw Guido toiling up the path.

McCreary went to meet him at a run.

"What's news, Guido? Good or bad? Did you see her? Were you able to get a message . . . ?"

Guido waved him away with weary humour.

"The news is good, *compar'*—most of it. I didn't see her, but I got a message to her. And if I don't have a wash and a beer right now, you'll never hear the rest of it! *Che brutta giornata!* What a hell of a day!"

They hustled him down to the creek and waited while he sluiced the dust off himself. Then they walked him swiftly back to the hut, poured a brace of drinks into him and sat, bent over the cane table under the hanging lamp, while he laid out in order the day's discoveries.

Guido's narrative style was vivid and theatrical, but his eye for detail was sharp and accurate.

". . . First we go in, the same as on the night of the big *festa*, only this time it is daylight and I see what goes. The gates are teak, twelve feet high and topped with spikes. All the front wall is wide, like a rampart, and the guards walk along the top. They have long guns, like you saw. God knows if they ever fire, but it is the kris that I should fear. Now the gardens—just terrace and steps between. They take me up through the same entrance—carved doors, open but guarded, one man either side. Now I am inside. It is an entrance so . . ." He sketched it swiftly in plan. "To the left, screen doors guarded. I find later these lead to the Sultan's apartments and, above him, to the rooms of the courtiers. Now, we get this first. It took me time to work out, but it is important. The ground floor and everything in it is for the Sultan—his personal apartments, the reception rooms, the women's rooms and the kitchens. All the others are upstairs—two, three floors, because the Navel of the Universe mustn't do anything so strenuous as walk up steps. Now, we come to it. I am to fix the lights in the big hall where the throne is—it makes a show when the Sultan is there with all his court. Also I think it frightens him to have such novelties in his private rooms. A disappointment, but I remember that there is the screen and behind it the women's quarters. Then I try to explain that I must find a place for the motor and generator. They smile and chatter, but make no sense to me. Then, at last, they take me out into the garden, not the women's garden, but the terrace below it, so I can see the wall and the big tree. I set the machines, then I run the lead along the top of the wall to give myself a look inside. I also measure the drop, and it is much like it looks through the glasses. Anyone can get out by climbing the big tree and going over the wall, but to get in is hard without a rope and a hook."

"You mean, Lisette could get out herself?"

"*Sicuro!*" Guido nodded vigorously. "And if there is someone on the outside to meet her, it is easier still."

"Go on!"

"Then I go inside to wire the hall. I make a messy job of it—hang the flex from pillar to pillar, with naked bulbs between—but nobody cares. It's beautiful, they think. And while I work, I sing, loud and clear, so that at first they think I'm mad, and afterwards they start to laugh. I make up a song to go with the music of 'Marechiare,' and I tell of a girl who goes every night after dark into a garden to watch the mountain where her lover will come and signal with a lamp, once, short and sharp, no more. Then I say that one day she has a message, and the same night the signal is three flashes, which means that her lover will come inside an hour and she must be ready to climb the tree and go over the wall to meet him. I sing it over and over, loud and clear, so that even on the ship they must have heard it."

"Let's hope they didn't," said McCreary. "What then? Did you get a reply?"

"I don't know what you'd call it," said Guido, with a

slow grin. "But after I finish, I hear giggling and talking behind the screen, and after a while a child comes out with a red flower in her hands and she says, loud and clear, but not knowing what it means: 'For the man.' Then I hear them laugh again, so I pat the head of the *bambina* and I give her my black flashlight for a return gift, an afterthought, but this way she can signal back to you. Then the men laugh, too, and everybody thinks I'm a *pazzo*, but nice. So they give me a drink and a plate of sweets which make me sick. I start up the engines, switch on the lights, show them how they work and know they don't understand. Then they give me a litter to take me back to the ship, and before I get here, I send the litter away and walk. And that's the news! Do you like it?"

"I like it fine!" said McCreary softly. "I like it more than anything I've heard for a long time. Pour the man another drink, Agnello. Pour him all the drink he wants. And when he's had dinner, I'm going to give him . . ."

"Oh, and another thing . . ." Guido's eyes were bright with malice. "Just to prove it really happened . . ."

He fished in the pocket of his shirt and brought out a small scarlet hibiscus, crushed and dying already, but still bright, and laid it in McCreary's palm.

"I think she would mean it for you. My voice isn't all that good, especially not in English."

"Thanks, *compar'*," said McCreary shakily. "*Mille, mille grazie!*"

Then Agnello took his pipe out of his mouth and said calmly, "Now, perhaps you can tell me something."

"What?" asked McCreary absently.

"Just this. You begin now to see a way to get yourself and your girl off the island. What happens then?"

"Murder!" said Guido, with relish. "Murder and riot. The Sultan's bride is stolen. *Mamma mia!* Then they call out the *guardia*—the boys with the wavy knives."

"That's right!" Agnello's long face grew longer still.

"And there is the *Corsair* in the harbour with a mixed crew of whites and Chinese and lascars and Malays. What happens to them? They are here—all except Rubensohn and Janzoon—as simple seamen. They have no part in this filthy business. What happens to them when the long knives come out and the villagers run amok in search of the Sultan's bride? Have you thought of that?"

"I've thought of it," said McCreary.

They looked at him, startled at the unfamiliar note in his voice.

The light from the lamp fell full on his face and they saw the lean, jutting jaw and the tight trap mouth and the shrewd Irish eyes that were not laughing anymore.

"You've thought of it," said Agnello flatly. "So . . . ?"

"So now I'll tell you. And every day and every night for the next weeks you'll ponder it waking and dream it sleeping, so that when the time comes, you won't make a single mistake."

Then they bent, tense and attentive, across the bamboo table, and he told them exactly what would happen the day the well came in.

# Chapter Fifteen

Three days later they began to drill.

Rubensohn wanted to make a ceremony of the spudding in: muster the officers and crew, bring down the Sultan and his court, bring out champagne, and then start the motors and watch the bits gouge in for the first time. There was a streak of the dramatist in him and a perverted humour.

McCreary rejected the idea out of hand. He was less than polite about it.

"Look, Rubensohn, if this were a normal project, sure! It makes a nice job for the publicity boys, keeps the shareholders happy, the stock market lively. But this isn't normal. It's a very dirty piece of grand larceny that started with a murder. You want your oil, I'm trying to get it for you. Why waste a day with this sort of humbug? If you want to get rid of your champagne, send it up to me. I'll have a lot of time on my hands to drink it."

Rubensohn looked at him sharply and then shrugged.

"Just as you please, of course. You're the boss. But why so prickly about it? Are you worried about something?"

"You're damn right I'm worried." McCreary was determined not to spare him a moment of anxiety. "Any one of these tremors could topple the rig, and we'd have to start again from scratch. If they get any worse, they could cave in the well and we'd lose our bits and our casing."

"Do you think they will get worse?"

"How should I know? I warned you, I can provide against technical hitches, but not against acts of God. If you watch that mountain up there, you'll see it's hotter and brighter than it was when we first came. That's normal, too—it's a kind of safety valve. But it's what goes on under the ground that starts the trouble."

Rubensohn frowned and turned away. McCreary grinned sourly at his retreating back. The man was sweating under the fans. There was no insurance on a job like this, and he had a lot of money on the table. That was the trouble with a crooked game. The jackpot was big, but a man could grow ulcers waiting for the draw. McCreary knew. He was in the game himself.

So, when they started the motors and the big bit began chewing the soft topsoil, there were only McCreary and Agnello and Rubensohn and Janzoon, with the girls and a gaggle of workmen. After they had watched for a while, McCreary led them back to the huts, poured them drinks and said crisply:

"From here on, it's a waiting game. You'll be anxious, so will I, but I don't want to be bothered with anything but tending the rig. Agnello can come every third day to check the motors and dress the tools. Send me up a typewriter from the ship and some graph paper. I'll write up a daily log and plot the drilling progress on a chart that corresponds with the surveyors' elevation. I'll send it down each morning by runner, so you'll know what's going on. Guido will call me morning and evening on the buzzer for any other messages. If I want anything from the ship, it's up to you to see that I get it smartly. For the rest, I want to be left alone. Is that clear?"

"Quite clear," said Rubensohn. "But you'll be up here a long time. Won't you need some company?"

McCreary grinned.

"I'll have Flame Flower—and Miranha, if I develop a taste for dirty stories. When Agnello comes up, he can stay the night. For the rest, I might do some fishing, I might take a few walks, and, if I'm still lonely, I'll invite myself to dinner on board."

"Do that," said Rubensohn genially. "We'll be happy to see you."

"I'm sure you will," said McCreary.

"Will you be working all night, too?" asked Janzoon.

"I won't," said McCreary, "but the plant will be. You'll be able to look up at night and see the lights on the derrick and think of the millions you'll have when it blows in."

"You'll have them, too, McCreary," said Rubensohn tartly. "Don't forget that."

"I won't forget," said McCreary. "I'll be thinking of them all the time."

When they had gone, he stood in the middle of the clearing and listened to the steady thud of the motors and saw the long steel spindle like a shining needle plunging down from the peak of the derrick. There was satisfaction in it, the deep, simple satisfaction of the professional. But it was marred by the thought that this was one project that would never grow beyond its infancy. There would be no pipelines running down to the water, no clutter of storage tanks and pumping stations, no town springing up on the harbour fringe, no ships in the bay. The derrick would rust in the monsoon rains and the jungle would surge back and devour the small impermanent relics of his stay.

When night came, he climbed once again to the neck of the valley from which Guido and he had first looked down on the palace. He carried the field glasses slung round his neck and a flashlight in his pocket. He set a brisk pace and timed the journey meticulously: twenty-three minutes.

When he reached the shelter of the two boulders, he lay down on his belly and scanned the garden and the colonnades behind it. There were lights in the palace, but the garden and the colonnades were all in darkness. If Lisette were there, he could not hope to see her.

He took the light out of his pocket, thrust it out, clear of the rocks and the undergrowth, and flicked it on. A second, no more—then he flicked it off again. He waited, his heart pounding, then from the shadows of the garden came a faint pinprick of light, like a lonely star. It was gone so quickly he might have dreamed it, but it told him what he wanted. Lisette was there. She had had the message. She had Guido's flashlight. She would wait and wait till he was ready to take her.

He raised the glasses again and swept the shadowy area that lay between his aerie and the wall of the garden. A mile and a half perhaps—no more. But there were no paths and the jungle grew thickly with undergrowth and trailing vines. It would close over his head like a canopy and he would have to navigate by the gradient of the land. It would need practice—one trip and another and another, till he had made a track for himself and had reduced the time to the lowest possible. When the final night came, time would be the deciding factor. Once Lisette's flight had been discovered, the alarm would be raised and the island would swarm like an anthill with searchers.

Well, this was the beginning of it. He stood up, scanned the hills again and tried to lay himself a course up the slope and down again, to end under the wall of the enclosed garden. Then he moved off. A minute later the jungle had swallowed him up.

It took him eighty minutes of sweating misery to make the trip. Trailing vines caught at his ankles, moss-grown logs crumpled under his feet, thorns tore at his clothes and whipping branches scratched at his cheeks. Roosting birds clattered in alarm and monstrous insects flicked angrily in front of his face. His body was streaming with perspiration and his nostrils were filled with the stench of rotting vegetation.

When, finally, he saw the dripping stones of the wall, he realized with a shock of terror that he was a hundred feet below his objective and that a guard with a long musket was standing on the parapet high above him. He crept back into the undergrowth like a frightened animal, and it took him another fifteen minutes to scramble up to the place where the big magnolia hung from the parapet.

He listened. There was no sound from the garden, only a faint tinkle of gamelan music from far inside the palace. He looked up at the dank, mossy stones of the wall. It was better than it looked from a distance—ten feet, no more. The branches were almost low enough for a man to leap and hold and hoist himself to the top of the wall. He fought against a wild impulse to try it then and there. Lisette was so near, yet he could not come to her, dared not even raise his voice to call her.

He looked at his watch, then turned back into the sweating shadows of the jungle.

When he reached the camp, he found Flame Flower squatting outside his hut, her eyes wide and terror-stricken. He had been away nearly four hours. With luck and practice, he thought he could get it down to two and a half. If he couldn't, their chances of survival were cut to a minimum.

He walked down to the creek to bathe and change into clean clothes, and when he came back Flame Flower had his meal ready. She squatted at his feet while he ate, and when he had finished, she brought him a cigarette and lit it for him. The little trick with the lighter never failed to amuse her, but tonight her small child's face was troubled.

She looked at him a moment and then said hesitantly, "Tuan?"

"Yes, little one. What is it?"

"Now that the other tuan is gone, do I sleep here with you?"

McCreary looked at her with grave, gentle eyes. She was young and ripe and perfect as a tropic flower, and he was alone and susceptible to comfort. He had lived and loved lightly enough in his time. Why hesitate now? He could take her, without question. She was a prince's gift, at his own disposal. He could use her and leave her with child and forget her, like all the other filibusters whose offspring people the islands and the Asian coasts. Lisette would not blame him. There was no one else to care. Only himself, and he did care, strangely and strongly. He had a momentary vision of her, on the night of the knives, haled before the Sultan's torturers, with McCreary's child in her belly.

But how to explain it to her in his halting Malay? How to make her understand without shame to her and danger to himself and Lisette? He said carefully:

"Do you know where I went tonight, little one?"

"Where, tuan?"

"I walked a long way through the jungle."

"No, tuan!" Her hand went to her mouth. "The spirits of the dead are abroad in the jungle and the Goddess of Death rides on a striped beast."

It was an odd echo of the old Hindu beliefs distorted, but persistent still in the scattered islands.

McCreary nodded.

"I walked through the jungle and I came to the wall of the Sultan's garden, and I heard my sister weeping on the other side. I dared not call to her. I could only sit and listen. After a while she went away."

"What then, tuan?" Her eyes were bright with sympathy.

"I swore a vow to my gods that I would not touch a

woman until my sister was taken away from the palace and given back to me again."

"But that will never happen, tuan. No woman leaves the palace, ever."

"This one will. One night she will leave and I shall take her away from Karang Sharo, and I shall take you with me, where the Sultan will never find us."

"Do you swear that, tuan?"

"I swear it."

"Then—then—if I may not come to you, may I sleep here in your hut? When I am alone and the ground shakes, I am frightened."

McCreary grinned at her and patted her sleek, perfumed hair. He said in English, "Whatever I do, you're a thorn in my flesh, little one. I suppose you might as well move in."

"What did you say, tuan?"

"I said, I would take you away, little one. Does that make you happy?"

"So long as I am near the tuan, I am happy."

He thought that if every woman in the world were like that, things would be a lot easier for the men in it. He undressed and lay down on the bed, and Flame Flower crawled into Agnello's bunk.

For a long time McCreary lay wakeful, listening to her soft, regular breathing and to the steady, thudding beat of the motors driving the drill. Then he fell asleep, exhausted. There were two more slight tremors during the night, but neither he nor Flame Flower wakened, and in the morning he found the rig still intact and the bit still clawing its way down through the first rock layer.

In the weeks that followed, McCreary's days patterned themselves into a comforting professional routine. He rose early and bathed in the stream, then walked back to the hut where Flame Flower would serve him his breakfast. Guido would call him on the radio, and they would chat back and forth on the keys, cautiously, for fear of eavesdroppers on the ship.

No messages were being received by Rubensohn, except a cable to the company in Singapore asking them to replenish bunker credits for the *Corsair* in Luzon and Hong Kong. McCreary let it pass without comment. The credits might come in handy later.

After the morning transmission he would go down the rig, fuel and tune the motors and direct the small team of Sharo recruits whom he had kept on the rig. They learnt quickly, he found. Their hands were apt at mechanical skills and, with a smile and a little flattery, they could be handled very easily.

As the bits went deeper and deeper and the casing followed them, McCreary began to take core samples, checking them against the geologist's survey for variations in the strata.

At night he would mark up the log and the chart, then he would tramp up the slope to the observation post and signal to Lisette—only once. Then, when he had seen the small answering light, he would plunge into the jungle again and time his walk back and forth from the garden wall. After half a dozen trips he found he could strike a bearing accurately and make the return journey in two and a half hours. He began to think of getting it down to two.

On the evenings when Miranha came to pick up his cans of fuel, McCreary would walk down to the beach with him and spend an hour fishing in the placid water between the shore and Miranha's mooring.

Miranha had prized two more bottles of whisky out of him, and now there was a dugout canoe beached under the bushes and ready for his use at all times. It was big and awkward for one man to handle, but, when the time came, it would have to carry a full load.

Every third day Agnello came up and spent the

daylight dressing the used bits and tuning the motors and checking the electrical circuits. After the evening meal he would walk up to the observation post with McCreary and wait for him to come back from the palace wall. Then they would sit in the hut and drink beer and smoke placidly, turning over their plans for the final day.

Agnello had made a new ally—the young deck officer, Arturo. They would need him on the final night. For the rest, the news from the ship was negligible. Rubensohn spent much time in his cabin, writing and studying McCreary's reports. Janzoon and Alfieri were at daggers drawn, and the girls were proving more of a nuisance than a recreation.

McCreary chuckled happily at Agnello's dry reportage. He knew how Rubensohn's temper must fray under the waiting. He regretted only that he couldn't string it out to breaking point.

One thing was worrying them all, it seemed—the volcano.

It was more active now than at any time since their arrival. Sometimes they would hear it grumbling, a low, thunderous sound, like a giant snoring in his sleep. At night a bright red glow lit the cone, and sometimes they would see a fiery shower blown high into the air and spreading out like sparks from a Roman candle. The tremors were slighter now, but more frequent, and there had been radio reports of severe shock waves in other areas.

"It may not mean much." Agnello sucked his pipe and talked in his calm, flat voice. "Etna plays up like this sometimes. Stromboli is always growling. But if it does . . . Mother of God!"

"Let's forget it!" said McCreary, uncomfortably, "and hope we're miles away when it does blow."

But he couldn't forget it, and more than once he woke from a shouting nightmare in which he saw the mountain spill over with fire and engulf the palace and the gardens, while Lisette's voice screamed for help, and he was held back from her by invisible hands.

Finally, one afternoon, a new core sample was brought up. It was black and porous and it looked like a crust of old cement. As he fumbled it, it left a brown, tarry stain on his hands. McCreary looked at it a long time, his lips moving soundlessly, his heart pounding. He knew what it was. He'd seen it before, many times.

The bits had driven down into an old porous layer which sometimes covers the main oil bed and sometimes is the oil bed. To bring in the well, it would be necessary to lower a long section of casing loaded with steel-jacketed bullets. When these were fired by electrical contact, the crust would break up, releasing the oil and sending it gushing to the surface. The surveyors had been right. Rubensohn's gamble had been right. There was oil on Karang Sharo, and tomorrow Mike McCreary would bring in his well. Tomorrow!

For the rest of the afternoon and long after sunset, McCreary drove his crew with a madman's energy. The drill was stopped and winched to the surface. The long steel bullets were loaded into the firing casing and the contents fused. The casing was lowered slowly down the shaft, and, when this was done, McCreary ran a long pair of cable leads to his own hut and carried the contact box there, too, and stowed it under his bed.

Then he dismissed the boys and stood a long time staring at the big derrick with its naked struts crisscrossed against the stars. Tomorrow!

But even tonight there was much to be done. He switched on the radio, put on the headphones, and after a few moments he heard Guido's impatient signal. He was late for his schedule.

"Tomorrow . . ." He tapped out the letters with trembling fingers. "Warn Agnello. Come yourself in the afternoon, early. No word to anyone. That's all. No more tonight."

"Understood," Guido's message came back. "Understood." And McCreary knew he could rely on them. They had been pondering it for a long time.

He sat down at his table, drew the typewriter towards him and, slowly and painstakingly, began to tap out the letters. There were two long documents and one very short one. When he had finished, he folded them carefully and put them in his wallet, which he placed under his pillow. Tomorrow!

Flame Flower brought him his meal and he ate it, sweating and filthy as he was, and drank two bottles of beer and smoked three cigarettes.

He took out his gun and oiled it and tested the action carefully, loaded it, put on the safety catch and placed it under the pillow with his wallet. Tomorrow!

Now he was deathly tired. His head was buzzing and his hands were trembling, and his whole body reeked with fatigue. He walked down to the creek to bathe himself and Flame Flower followed him, and, when he stepped under the racing cool water, she came with him and soaped and sluiced his body with her soft hands, dried him and led him back to the hut walking like a man in a dream.

When they reached the hut, she urged him to lie down and sleep, but he refused. He lifted her onto the table and perched her in front of him and told her, very carefully, what she herself must do when tomorrow came. How she must go to the palace and to the apartments of the women and entertain them with her stories of life with the tuan, and how she must say to Lisette, foolishly, as if it were a child's mimicry: "Tonight . . . three lights . . . wait!"

He made her say it over and over again, like a parrot, so that there could be no mistake. Then he told her how she must leave the palace early in the afternoon and come back to him to confirm that Lisette had his message. She nodded wisely, and he made her repeat the directions slowly and carefully; when he asked for the words again, she gave them to him clearly and without hesitation:

"Tonight . . . three lights . . . wait!"

Now there was nothing more for him to do, until tomorrow. He lay down on the bed, fully clothed, and fell instantly asleep. But Flame Flower heard him muttering and wrestling with his nightmares, and she came to him and soothed him with crooning voice and soft hands, and, after a while, she lay down on the sheets beside him and cradled his head on her breasts, so that even when the tremors came, he did not hear them, and when he woke again it was already—tomorrow!

# Chapter Sixteen

The Sharo boys came straggling up the hill, laughing and chattering as they always did. McCreary set them restacking the stores, polishing the engines, cutting new timber—everything he could find to keep them busy and create an illusion of normal activity.

When Miranha came up, blear-eyed and inquisitive as a weasel, McCreary took him up to the hut and told him what he wanted of him. The fellow's eyes started from his head and his mouth gaped with the shock of it.

"Mother of pity! I can't do it. You know what this means? Ruin for me! I lose everything."

"You've got a hut and a clutter of trade junk!" said McCreary brutally. "I'll replace it for you two over. You've got a wife and children I can't replace and your own worthless throat that I wouldn't replace, if I could. If you stay, you'll be murdered. If you try to double-cross me, I'll kill you myself. Make up your mind!"

"No . . . no . . . no!" Miranha was gibbering with terror. "Anything you say. But you'll pay me for the boat, give me a new start?"

"Yes! Now, listen carefully. Get your wife and kids onto the ketch—not yet, late in the afternoon! Then come up here. If you're not here by sunset, I'll send Guido gunning for you. Is that clear?"

"Clear, yes . . . but how can you be sure?"

"I am sure," said McCreary. "I've got to be sure. Now get to hell out of here and be back by sunset. I want you to take a message down to the ship."

McCreary watched him shambling down the path, then he turned back to Flame Flower. Swiftly he led her once more through the catechism. She answered him without hesitation, and the four words she must speak to Lisette came back to him clear as a bell. Then she, too, left him and his heart followed her small colourful figure flashing like a parrot's plumage under the first green overhang of the jungle.

Shortly after noon Guido arrived, sweating and excited.

"Big things, *amico! Festa* day! And on the ship they doze and drink and snarl at each other as if it were any other day of the month. The mountain worries them. They don't like the way it rumbles and spits. I laugh at them and tell them how old Vesuvio blew his top. They like that—like poison. Their eyes pop and they give themselves indigestion worrying about it."

"They won't have to worry about it much longer, Guido. Tonight will see the end of it."

"I hope so," said Guido, with fervour. "Even for me it gets too much."

"Everything set on the ship?"

"Everything. Agnello and young Arturo are primed. They know the movements, the timetable."

"The timetable—everything depends on that."

"Everything," said Guido.

They sat down to go over it again.

Just after four, Flame Flower came back. She had been to the women's quarters. They had welcomed her and petted her and listened avidly to her stories of the tuans

184

and their strange ways. She had recited her little words to
Lisette and the other women had laughed at the mimicry,
not understanding a sound of it.

When she had left, they had given her presents, fruits
and sweetmeats and a comb for her hair and a bracelet for
her wrist. Lisette had given her a cambric handkerchief,
scented with her perfume. Her message was written on the
handkerchief in bright red lacquer.

"Mike, come early. Two hours after sunset latest."

McCreary smiled thinly. Two hours after sunset and
she should be back here, in the hut, waiting for Rubensohn
and Janzoon. There were no margins in the schedule. He
hoped and prayed that Rubensohn and Janzoon would
arrive on time.

At five o'clock they dismissed the Sharo boys, and
within ten minutes the clearing was deserted.

At five-thirty Miranha arrived, red-eyed and unhappy.
His family was aboard the ketch. He, himself, would like to
join them. He was worried . . . he had no talent for this
sort of thing . . . they were sure of their promise to make
good his losses and give him a new start . . . ?

They were sure. They were even surer that they would
kill him if he lost his nerve. McCreary sat down and wrote a
brief note to Rubensohn.

"Drilling site tonight. Urgent conference, self, Janzoon. Expect good news. McCreary."

He folded it and handed it to Miranha.

"You'll leave here at six by Guido's watch. At normal
going, you'll be aboard before seven. Don't dawdle, don't
hurry, and above all don't be diverted by anything. If you
make a mistake in timing, we're all dead men. Understand
that."

Miranha understood, but he needed liquor and cigarettes and a mixture of threats and encouragement to
bolster his small courage.

It was twenty minutes to six when McCreary himself

set off up the mountain path to his observation post. In his pockets he carried the flashlight and the gun. The field glasses were slung round his neck, and, looped over his shoulders, mountaineer fashion, was a length of rope, with a large grappling hook at the end of it. Agnello had made it for him, covering the hook with rubber tubing so that it would not clatter against the stonework.

He walked swiftly up the slope, thinking of Lisette, thinking of all that must be done in the next hours, and how a few minutes could make the difference between success and disaster.

By the time he reached the rocks, the swift-striding dark had come down on the island and the cone of Gurung Merapi glowed angrily against the night sky. There was a deep rumbling and the hills shuddered under his feet, then settled again, slowly. From the cone of the volcano a fountain of fire erupted, then fell back again through the smoke.

He stood upright against the rocks, holding the glasses in one hand and the light in the other. Carefully, as if aiming a gun, he thrust it out beyond the rocks and flashed it— once, twice and again. The answer came back swiftly this time. Three short flashes, magnified a little by the glasses, but still small and uncertain, like his own hope.

He put the flashlight in his pocket and set off down the slope and into the jungle. The way was more familiar to him now, its hazards fewer. Long practice had given him the feel of the ground, and his quickened senses led him now to this fallen trunk, round that tangle of lianas, down the dip and over the hump and past the sound of water on the left. . . .

Panting and staggering, he came to the base of the wall and leaned against it, fighting for breath. He looked at his watch. He had covered the full distance in forty minutes. The margin was a mite better, but he could not afford to waste it.

He eased his way up the slope to where the big magnolia tree hung over the wall. The ground was slippery with the drainage from the hill and he had to go carefully or risk a crashing tumble down the slope.

He unslung the rope and paid out a length of it from the coil, holding the covered hook in his hands. He tried one throw, but he was too cautious and the hook fell back at his feet with a soft thud. He tried another; the hook hung on the wall, but when he put weight on it, the lip of the wall crumbled in a shower of loose rubble. McCreary splayed himself against the stones, trembling. No sound came from the garden, only the distant muted noise of the falling fountain.

Carefully, he tried again. This time the hook held. He tested it with a strong pull, and another, and another. It was still firm. He eased his weight onto it and began to hoist himself up the wall under the shadow of the branches.

When he reached the top, he hung there, peering into the garden through the small gaps in the leaves.

A moment later his heart stood still.

The Sultan, himself, was in the garden, and Lisette was with him, walking slowly by the fountain under the blossom trees.

He dared not hoist himself up any farther. He could not go back for fear that Lisette might leave the garden without his knowing it. He hung there, bracing himself on the rope, till his muscles screamed and the sweat broke out all over him and he had to bite his lips to keep from crying out. The ticking of his watch was loud as a death knell, and he knew that both time and strength were slipping away from him.

Then they stopped walking. The small brown figure of the Sultan turned away, then came back, as if on an afterthought. He talked a few moments in a low voice and Lisette bent her head in acknowledgment. Then, abruptly, he turned on his heel and walked swiftly through the colonnade, leaving Lisette alone.

McCreary eased himself a little higher on the rope and struggled to find breath enough for a whistle. It issued from his lips with startling shrillness. He saw Lisette's head turn sharply. She cast a quick, scared look towards the lighted colonnade, then moved unhurriedly towards the big magnolia tree.

"Is that you, Mike?" Her voice was a whisper, but he heard it louder than drums.

"It's me, dark one." His own voice was strained and harsh. "Up into the tree now—hurry!"

He stayed long enough to see her safely into the first branches, holding his breath lest the dry snapping of twigs should bring them running and screaming after her. Then he slid down the rope and waited, tense as a spring, until he saw her, like a white moth, coming over the wall and out of the dark leaves.

"Jump, sweetheart! I'll catch you!"

He saw her hesitate a moment, then she jumped. The impact rolled him over on the slippery incline, but he was on his feet in an instant and, without a kiss or come-hither, he was dragging her into the shadows and stumbling with her over the rotting floor of the jungle.

Before they had gone half a mile, she was gasping and retching with fatigue. McCreary brought up short and held her to him, taking her weight on his breast and shoulders, feeling her small body wrenched with sobbing weariness. He looked at his watch. Three minutes after seven. No time to spare, if they were to be back before Rubensohn arrived.

He lifted her face to him and kissed her gently. Then he spoke swiftly and sharply.

"Listen, Lisette. Time's against us. We've an hour to be back in the camp and then maybe half an hour of comedy that you must see out, because I've prepared it for you and no other. Then we'll kiss the backs of our hands to this place and be on our way. I'll carry you pickaback part of the way, then I want you to walk, and walk with all the strength you've got. Don't fail me now, dark one! You won't, will you? Tell me you won't!"

"I—I won't, Mike."

"That's my fine dark woman."

He hoisted her onto his shoulders and carried her a little way until her strength came back, then she walked, plugging and persistent, behind him, until they came to the camp, with ten minutes to spare before Rubensohn and Janzoon arrived.

Guido laughed and stammered and swore and patted them both on the shoulders, while Flame Flower stood goggling at the tattered apparitions. McCreary rounded on them impatiently.

"That's enough! Both of you! Time, remember! Time! Get Lisette into the other hut, Flame Flower. Help her to clean up, lend her clean clothes. I'm sorry, sweetheart, but I want you looking like a queen when Rubensohn comes, for all you're dead on your small, brave feet!"

"I'll be ready, Mike!" Her head went up proudly and the weariness seemed to fall away from her.

"Stay in the hut till I come for you. Don't move outside. Hurry now! Guido!"

"Yes, *amico?*"

"Connect the plunger box."

"I've done it, Mike—it's just outside the door. I thought you'd want it there."

"Good! There's a bundle of assorted stones and jade in my bag. Take it and give it to Flame Flower. Tell her to bring it with her when we go down to the boat."

"Yes, Mike. Anything else?"

"Yes, Guido." His voice was soft now and very deliberate. "There'll be a small ceremony when they come. I want no risks at all. If Rubensohn makes half a move, kill him! No questions, no hesitations. Kill him!"

"A pleasure, *compar'*," said Guido, feelingly. "A very great pleasure indeed."

McCreary grinned crookedly and went into the hut. It took him three minutes flat to change and clean himself, and when Rubensohn and Janzoon came tramping up the hill, he was waiting for them, cool as bog water, with a cigarette stuck in his mouth and the light of triumph in his eyes.

"Well, McCreary?" Rubensohn's voice was shrill and edgy. His eyes were bright with anticipation and his red lips were startlingly vivid against his pale, perspiring face. "Your message said good news. We hope you'll make up for our spoiled dinner."

"I think you'll find it worth the trip," said McCreary, with a grin. "You'll forgive me for being a little elated myself. It's the Irish in me. Come in, gentlemen, and sit down."

He led them into the hut and sat them down at the bamboo table with their faces to the door of the hut. He made a little ceremony of it, so that they looked at him curiously, wondering if he'd been drinking. McCreary smiled and smiled and leaned against the bamboo upright of the door.

Then he said in his gentlest brogue, "Gentlemen, I have good news for you! I'm going to bring you in a well!"

"My God!" Rubensohn's voice was a high bat's squeak.

"You mean it!" Janzoon's voice was a hoarse whisper. "When?"

McCreary looked at his watch. Fifteen minutes after eight. Time was running out fast.

He said briskly, "Very soon now!! Tonight! You'll see me leaning on a plunger and you'll count three—or maybe five—and you'll see one of the most wonderful sights in the world: a gusher spouting black, filthy oil towards the stars. Does it please you, gentlemen?"

"So much!" Rubensohn chuckled shrilly. "You don't know how much, McCreary."

"But before I do that," said McCreary, "there's something else I want to show you, more wonderful to me than all the oil in the world." He raised his voice and shouted, "Guido!"

A moment later Guido stepped into the hut with Lisette.

Janzoon goggled at her open-mouthed. Rubensohn leapt up from his chair.

"Sit down, Rubensohn," said McCreary's soft voice. "Sit down or I'll kill you!"

Rubensohn saw the gun in his hand and death in his Irish eyes. He sat down. Lisette stood watching him, a small, queenly figure with a strange smile playing about her lips.

"You're mad!" cried Rubensohn shrilly. "You're raving mad! Any minute from now there'll be gongs beating from the palace and the whole island will come swarming over us, like soldier ants."

"I know," said McCreary. "I've thought about it—often. Take their guns, Guido!"

Guido moved swiftly round the table and came back with two guns. McCreary smiled his lopsided smile.

"So you were going to kill me? That makes it easier all round."

"Listen, McCreary . . ."

"Shut up, Rubensohn!" The smile was gone now and his mouth was tight with anger. "Cover them, Guido! If they move, kill 'em!"

"I know," said Guido, with a flashing smile. "I've thought about it too."

McCreary put his hand into his breast pocket and brought out a fountain pen and the folded typescripts over which he had laboured the night before. He opened them out and laid them on the table before Rubensohn.

"Sign the first two, please."

Rubensohn looked up at him with cold, hating eyes. "What am I supposed to sign?"

"The first is a will, which is to be witnessed by Guido and Agnello, leaving all your property, real and personal, to Lisette Morand, late of Saigon, except the *Corsair*, which comes to me because you owe me money and a lot else that you can't repay. The second is a confession, similarly witnessed, to your murder of Captain Nasa in Djakarta on the tenth of July."

"You're mad, McCreary! I'm not going to sign those."

McCreary looked at his watch.

"If you don't," said McCreary calmly, "Guido will shoot you both in five seconds from now. And I'll guarantee to have a signature out of you before you die."

"And if I do sign?"

"I'll bring your well in for you and you can both go back to the *Corsair*."

"Now I know you're mad!" said Rubensohn. "A will has no value until a man's dead."

"You're dead already," said McCreary very softly, "but you don't know it yet. I'm counting now. One . . . two . . ."

"Sign it, Rubensohn . . . for God's sake, sign!" Janzoon was sweating in his chair.

"Three . . . four . . ."

"Give me the pen!"

"I know your signature now, Rubensohn," said McCreary, easily, "so make sure it's the right one."

Rubensohn scrawled his signature on the first two documents. McCreary took them from him, folded them and put them back in his pocket.

"What's this?" Rubensohn was staring down at the last sheet of paper.

McCreary said coolly, "That's the message Guido's going to send to Scott Morrison in Darwin telling him

192

there's no oil on Karang Sharo and that the deal is off. And, as you see, it will be signed, like all the others, by Janzoon."

Rubensohn's face was ashen; for the first time since McCreary had known him, there was fear in his eyes and in his twitching lips.

"But . . . but there is oil here! You said . . ."

"I know," said McCreary. "I promised you oil and I'm going to give it to you—enough to choke you. Then I'm going to . . . Listen!"

They all heard it, a great throbbing brazen gong, echoing out across the lowlands from the palace on the hill. It went on and on, rising into the hills and falling into the valleys of sound, and from the villages there rose a shrill crying like the wailing of lost souls.

"That's it!" said McCreary. "The alarm. The Sultan's wife has disappeared. Twenty minutes from now they'll be scouring the island. It should be interesting. You'll both be here to watch it. Then, of course, you'll be taken and killed. At this moment the *Corsair* is steaming out of the harbour with young Arturo at the wheel and Agnello down in the engine room and Alfieri beating his head against his door. If I can talk sense into him in the next day or two, maybe I'll give him the command after all, Janzoon!"

Then the full horror of their situation seemed to dawn on Rubensohn and Janzoon. They gaped, slack-mouthed, and Janzoon tried to lurch forward, but Guido thrust him back. Rubensohn burst into a gibbering plea:

"For God's sake, McCreary! Listen! I'll give you . . ."

"You've got nothing to give me," said McCreary. "Stripjack naked! The game's over, Rubensohn! You're busted! And here's a small souvenir of the moment—Nasa's lighter! I took it from his body."

He tossed the lighter on the table. Then, while Rubensohn still stared at it, he turned and led Lisette out of the hut. Guido brought the others out with a beckoning jerk of the pistol.

The island was still full of the clangour of the great gong, but McCreary stood steady as a rock with his hand on the plunger, and Lisette was beside him, head high and proud.

"Watch it!" said McCreary exultantly. "Watch it! Count three or maybe five and you'll see it come—the thing you killed a man for and sold a girl for, the thing you're going to die for, Rubensohn—oil!"

His hand went down on the plunger and they waited, one . . . two . . . but before the count was done, the ground rocked under their feet and they heard a noise louder than a hundred gongs and, as they staggered on their feet, they saw that the top of the mountain had blown off and the air was full of flying particles, as if from a blasted sun tumbling out of the sky.

Then they were running, helter-skelter down the path, McCreary dragging Lisette, Guido with Flame Flower at his heels and Janzoon and Rubensohn stumbling after them, shouting, as explosion after explosion rocked the ground and the fiery missiles rained down like thunderbolts.

The path gave them a small shelter from the red-hot lapilli, but they could hear them clattering and hissing among the arching trees, and if one brushed them as it fell, it scorched them so that they cried out with the pain of it.

When they reached the path that led back to the village, they saw for a brief moment the growing terror of the situation. All along the coastline the kampongs were ablaze as the fallout from the explosions touched off the grass roofs like torches.

They saw the flames and heard the wild, panic screaming, then McCreary dragged them off the path and through the last green tangle before the sea.

The four of them reached the beach fifty yards ahead of

Rubensohn and Janzoon. The sea was in a turmoil, tossing wildly and roaring like storm water. They could see the ketch heaving and straining at its anchor, but Miranha was cowering under the bushes, staring with terror. They kicked him out of his stupor and between them they manhandled the canoe down the sand and into the water.

As they climbed into it and pushed off, Rubensohn and Janzoon broke out of the bushes and onto the beach.

"McCreary!" It was Rubensohn's voice, high and despairing.

McCreary did not turn his head. He and Guido bent to the paddles and sent the canoe bouncing out across the waves to where the ketch was straining at its anchor in the lurching water.

"McCreary! McCreary!"

They were both shouting now, their voices shrill with terror, and, when at last he turned his head, he could see them wading out, waist-high, into the water.

It was desperate, back-breaking labour to hold the plunging craft head on to the waves and save it from being swamped. But after an eternity of clawing their way through the surf, they brought up under the lee of the ketch. When they scrambled aboard, they found Miranha's wife and children screaming in panic, but McCreary drove Miranha like a maniac.

"Get those damned engines started! Guido, get the anchor up! The rest of you get down below, if you don't want to be burnt! Hurry! Hurry! Hurry!"

Red-hot pellets were raining down on the deck, and already it was beginning to smoulder. The ketch was bucking like a wild horse as great shudders shook the sea floor and tossed the waves higher and higher. Guido was straining and cursing to get the anchor up. It seemed an age till McCreary heard the splutter of the engines and Guido's shout and felt the boat yaw drunkenly at the first drive of the screws.

The sea was chopping all ways at once, but when the big waves broke over the decks, they were grateful for it, as for a small mercy, because the smouldering pellets doused themselves and the new falls spluttered out in the wash.

Miranha was driving the engines full throttle now and the little boat was thrusting out, bucking and yawing, towards the lights of the *Corsair*, miles to seaward.

McCreary stood in the stern looking back at the shoreline where Rubensohn and Janzoon stood neck-deep now, still shouting their desperate plea.

"McCreary! McCreary!"

Then a new shower of blazing particles rained down, and their voices trailed off in a long-drawn scream of agony, quickly quenched as the wild waters swallowed them.

I've stripped him down, he thought. I've stripped him down to this—a face I can't see and a voice drowned in a few seconds. I've taken his girl. I've taken his money. I've taken his life. And though I don't feel very proud of myself, I'm damned if I can feel any pity for him.

Then they rounded the small cape and saw for the first time the blazing horror of the spectacle. The volcano was still spouting fire and roaring like a mad giant, the air was full of a stinking sulfurous smoke and the whole of the shoreline was blazing as if it had been sprayed with gasoline.

The brown people were scurrying like ants, in a panic stampede to the water. Even above the roaring of the mountain, their cry was a high shriek across the leaping waves.

"Dear God Almighty!" McCreary's voice was a hoarse whisper.

"Mike! Mike! Can't we do something for them?" Lisette was at his shoulder, steadying herself against the yaw. "Can't we go back a way? Pick some of them up?"

McCreary shook his head and shouted to make her hear.

"We'd be burned and swamped in two minutes. Best we can do is stand in as close as we dare with the *Corsair* and try to pick up survivors. Look . . . !"

She followed his pointing finger and saw the first canoe loads pushing off from the beach and the small stubby praus lurching out into the water with people fighting to cling to their thwarts.

Before they were twenty yards from the beach, the water spun them up and around, spilling the bodies out like matches and dumping the heavy hulls down on their bobbing heads.

"It's horrible, Mike! Horrible!" She buried her face in his breast and he held her close to him, swaying with the boat as Miranha pushed and cursed her out towards the *Corsair.*

"Close your eyes to it, dark one," McCreary urged her desperately. "Close your eyes and shut your ears and your heart. You've had pain enough and this you can do nothing to mend. Hold to me, sweetheart, and you'll feel the soft, cool wind stirring over the grass, and you'll catch the pipe of the blackbird and hear the drumming of the hooves as the sweet fillies turn over the rise and come pounding homeward over the hills of Armagh. Listen to 'em, dark one! Listen. . . ."

But even as he spoke, they heard a sound like an enveloping thunderclap, and, as they watched, dumb with shock, they saw the whole hillside open up and a great river of fire slide slowly over the palace and down towards the villages and the sea.

## ABOUT THE AUTHOR

MORRIS WEST, a native Australian, was born in Melbourne in 1916. When he was fourteen he began studying as a postulant with the Christian Brothers order but left twelve years later without having taken final vows. After serving with Australian Army Intelligence during World War II, he became a partner in a flourishing recording and transcription business but left it when he discovered that he preferred to write for himself rather than for sponsors.

A stay in Italy resulted in his book *Children of the Sun*, a study of street urchins, which became an English best seller in 1957. There followed two novels published in the United States under the titles *The Crooked Road* and *Backlash*, in 1957 and 1958 respectively.

In 1958, also, Mr. West returned to Italy as Vatican correspondent for *The Daily Mail*, and he then absorbed much of the technical background for a new novel. *The Devil's Advocate*, published in 1959, promptly became that rare phenomenon in publishing—a book universally hailed by critics as a major creative work while selling, in various editions, more than two million copies. Mr. West followed it with more major successes: *Daughter of Silence* (1962). *The Shoes of the Fisherman* (1963). *The Ambassador* (1965), and *The Tower of Babel* (1967). He is also the author of *Harlequin*, *Proteus* and *The Clowns of God*.

Mr. West has lived in England and Italy, and presently lives in New South Wales, Australia.

# MORRIS WEST

If you liked this Morris West favorite, you'll want all these thrilling bestsellers.

| | | |
|---|---|---|
| ☐ 23305 | THE CONCUBINE | $3.50 |
| ☐ 23109 | THE AMBASSADOR | $3.50 |
| ☐ 22913 | HARLEQUIN | $3.50 |
| ☐ 20694 | DAUGHTER OF SILENCE | $2.95 |
| ☐ 20901 | SHOES OF THE FISHERMAN | $3.50 |
| ☐ 20662 | CLOWNS OF GOD | $3.95 |
| ☐ 20481 | BACKLASH | $3.50 |
| ☐ 14074 | PROTEUS | $3.50 |
| ☐ 20688 | TOWER OF BABEL | $3.50 |

# RELAX!
## SIT DOWN
## and Catch Up On Your Reading!

# THRILLERS

Gripping suspense . . . explosive action . . . dynamic characters . . . international settings . . . these are the elements that make for great thrillers. And Bantam has the best writers of thrillers today—Robert Ludlum, Frederick Forsyth, Jack Higgins, Clive Cussler—with books guaranteed to keep you riveted to your seat.